WHERE BEAUTIFUL INKS

WINTER

A POETIC ANTHOLOGY

EDITED BY:
BRANDY LANE

FORT WAYNE, INDIANA

ISBN: 978-1-7363268-2-4

LIBRARY OF CONGRESS CONTROL NUMBER: 2023903938

ALL PICTURES THROUGHOUT THIS BOOK ARE AVAILABLE
THROUGH CANVA AND CANVA PRO.

DEDICATION

This is dedicated to all of the poets that have come together in whatever season they are in, to celebrate, or mourn together in the pages of this book. Within these pages, you will find fond memories, fresh wounds, melancholy, and an unwavering sense of hope. You will find faith, both strong, and lost. I hope that as you winter-over this season, you find rest in what you know to be true, peace in the chaos of life, and rest for your weary souls. Whatever your religion, or wherever you are on this planet, I wish you abundant renewal when springtime comes.

TABLE OF CONTENTS

TABLE OF CONTENTS

TABLE OF CONTENTS

TABLE OF CONTENTS

TABLE OF CONTENTS

TABLE OF CONTENTS

TABLE OF CONTENTS

TABLE OF CONTENTS

TABLE OF CONTENTS

GRACE WAGNER

STEVIE FLOOD

WHERE BEAUTIFUL INKS

WINTER

A POETIC ANTHOLOGY

FOREWORD

This anthology of poetry and prose by poets from around the world delves into the many celebrations that begin early in the season and the doldrums and melancholy that winter can bring. There are themes dealing with Halloween, Thanksgiving, Christmas, New Year's Day, Valentine's Day, and Mother's Day. There are also themes dealing with love, family, memories, and loss, including the loss of a spouse, children, pets, parents, homes, and oneself. We all celebrate and grieve from every corner of the world. While winter may be snowy in one part of the world and stormy in another, and Christmas may be during a cold season in the North and warm in the South, we are all humans and can relate to each other on the simplest levels of joy and grief. On these basic levels, we can comfort and empathize with one another to get through the struggles of what seems cold and dark, just like the months we refer to as "winter." Each poet is represented by their dialect and word spelling to demonstrate where they are from. Every poet is housed in their own "chapter," which tells a little about them and their location. Curated and edited by Brandy Lane, of Where Beautiful Inks LLC, this is her first collaborative anthology.

With special thanks to Julie Keleher for her dedication and hours spent listening to me read poems over and over again to make sure that each one was exactly as it should be written. She has poured love into this book as a shepherd to the poets. I, for one, am grateful.

About the Author/Curator/Editor

Brandy Lane

Brandy Lane has lived most of her life in Indiana and Colorado, where she resides with her husband and four children. She published her first book, *Where Beautiful Loves*, in December 2020 under her imprint Where Beautiful Inks. Just after the release of her first book, she discovered anthologies as an option for publishing and has since had poetry pieces included in over three dozen publications. Publications include *Poetry 365 by RDW* (both abridged and unabridged editions) for November, December, January, February, March, April, May, and June, and special editions of *Creator* and *Self Portrait* editions. Red Penguin Books has published her pieces in *'Tis the Season's*, *The Flower Shop on the Corner*, and *The Ocean Waves*. Clarendon House Publications published her poems in their *Poetica 2* and *Poetica 3* anthologies, and her work was also included in Ink Gladiator's Press anthologies of *The Rise and Fall of Chimera's* and *Gray, We Hide our Colors Within*. Indie Blu(e) Publishing just published a mental health piece in *Through the Looking Glass: Reflecting on Madness and Chaos Within*, and their newest anthology, *But You Don't Look Sick: The Real Life Adventures of Fibro Bitches, Lupus Warriors, and Other Superheroes Battling Invisible Illness*. 300 South Media Group has published her in *As Darkness Falls* and features her first flash fiction piece in *Sunset Rain*. Train River Poetry has published her in *Poetry 7*. She also appears in *Who's Who of Emerging Writers* by Sweetycat Press. Most recently, she has been published by *Harness Magazine* in their November issue, and in Silent Spark Press *Amazing Poetry*. Brandy can be found online: on Instagram and Facebook @wherebeautifullives, @wherebeautifulloves, or her web page www.wherebeautifulinks.com

- AUTUMN'S VEIL
- BUTTERFLIES OF WINTER
- GRAY
- HALFWAY BLOOMING
- ALL I WILL EVER WANT
- WINTER, UP NORTH
- ALL AWASH IN CANDLELIGHT
- CHRISTMAS MEMORIES
- A BLANKET OF STARS

BRANDY LANE

The sun sinks on the horizon, beaming down its liquid gold—
its light reflecting off of leaves; their colors brash, and bold.

The light of day is waning, while trees clamor for the rays,
seeking nourishment they lack from summer's longer days.

Leaves blush crimson in the wind, caught in an embrace...
entwined in tango one last time as they fall from their place.

Autumn, adorned in color, as a bride on her big day;
her lustrous locks of brown and gold, with wispy streaks of gray.

Her luscious lips are the deepest red, her eyes, a maple hue,
and in the chill, her pumpkin cheeks grow rosy thru and thru.

She smells of apples and bonfire, with slight hints of fresh straw.
In all her glory, she is a sight! She'll leave you struck in awe.

She breezes down the aisle, stirring leaves with gentle grace.
As they perform their final dance, they slowly die, in place.

The animals bow in tribute to the queen that they adore...
thanking her for the bounty, they have placed in winter stores.

Frost, in the form of Autumn's veil, intricately sewn...
appears on all that breathed the light, that will again be grown.

WINTER

Covering their demise in such a glorious shimmer of light
entombed in shards of crystal as-if-in armor for a fight.

Autumn advances toward her groom, a chill runs down her spine.
As temperatures drop, animals leave—for they've run out of time.

He sweeps her up to gaze at her with eyes of brightest blue,
she succumbs to breathlessness becoming quite subdued.

Wearing a tuxedo, dressed in white from head to toe,
when speaking, his exhalations turn to the whitest snow.

Autumn is seduced, she collapses in his arms...
she breathes her final breath—falling victim to his charms.

In Winter's sadness, skies turn gray, the winds grow rather cold.
Like magic, he's grown hair of white and looks to be quite old.

He howls with grief into the winds the veil has been torn.
A freeze takes all deciduous life—Oh! How Winter mourns!

Winter's heart is cold and deep, his mourning never fades,
but now and then you'll see a new veil he has made.

In mem'ry of how he adored his lovely bride, so frail...
you'll see the melancholy in the train of Autumn's veil.

BUTTERFLIES OF WINTER

The butterflies of winter,
swooping downward with an airy current,
only to land with whispers on the ground.

They flock to and fro,
from whence they come no one ever really sees,
but they come quietly, without a sound.

Impaled on the blades of grass,
they lie cold and still, piled together,
no longer capable to fly around.

Ephemeral whilst winds cold...
yet disappear with the warm air of spring,
absorbed by the extremely thirsty ground.

Hydrating the bulbs and roots,
the first feast of the fluttering flyers,
sweet nectar in abundance is found!

GRAY

This gray, melancholy day...
cold, and wet, and crying;
as if in mourning the fading fall;
the leaves and flowers are dying.

No longer adorned in their gowns,
the trees, now bare, are found;
their garments, scattered all over,
like dirty laundry on the ground.

Oh, the memory of just last week,
the pigments at their peak;
the sun shone brightly in the sky,
not like this, it's awfully bleak.

The windows down, I drove through town
and smiled at the sights;
but now it seems, 'twas all a dream,
as warmth has taken flight.

BRANDY LANE

Frozen in time
melancholy frost from
early autumn nights
that chill the air;
nipping harshly at my outer petals.

I cannot last without your warmth,
I will not survive without
your happy smile
beaming down on me.

Your time is less and less each day—
the time you spend with me.

The cold and lonely nights
are leaving me stranded,
stuck in time.

What will become of me without your
love, without you to chide me into
opening up?

I was so timid before,
but you comforted me into blossoming,
and I have grown so much inside.

Maybe my timing wasn't quite right,
because inside, I am bursting with so
much I want to give; my fragrance, my
beauty, my petals swaying on the
breeze to catch your attention.

HALFWAY BLOOMING

Alas, I fear you've gone too quickly,
I'm afraid I will only wilt away
on this cold and lonely night
without you here.

I nod my head in silence,
I can't take it anymore!

As I succumb to the sad realization
that you have left me...

halfway blooming.

ALL I WILL EVER WANT

Snowflakes bunched together,
cascading down in gentle thuds,
smashing on my eyelashes
and melting on my cheeks.

Christmas Eve services ended,
we walked to our cars,
marveling at the glistening crystals
glittering the streets.
It crunches under our feet.
One last hug before we go our separate ways.

I hold the large envelope in my hand.
"Do not open till Christmas morning!"
I don't need to open it at all,
although I will come morning.

I already got what I wanted for Christmas,
and for every Christmas yet to come!
It didn't come wrapped,
or with any pomp or circumstance,
but it is and always will be my favorite.

All I will ever want is you.

A kajillion stars,
frozen lakes as I have never witnessed,
darkest skies with puffy white clouds
that the stars shone around.

Pines to the sky,
silence enveloping me,
stillness—with a sense of being tiny,
yet overwhelmed at once.

Stiff waters,
ice covering the landscape for miles,
the moon, reflecting the sun's rays,
shimmers off of the glossy sheen.

I stood and took on the winds,
that were seemingly racing
to find somewhere to bump into—
nearly taking my breath.

No evidence of springtime here,
not underneath
the five or six feet of snow remaining,
although, a sense of rebirth is in the air.

I could stay in the wilderness forever...
but life beckons me back.
The constraints I've placed myself in
are evident now.

To be free like the birds,
the squirrels, the deer, and the moose.
But alas, a different sort of life
altogether is theirs.

The northern lights did not dance for me
this time and my soul longs to gaze upon them in
this lifetime...
someday.

WINTER, UP NORTH

ALL AWASH IN CANDLELIGHT

I want to write of last Christmas Eve,
but how do I properly capture
the moment burned into my memory?

Oh, to wander back in time one year!

The candles lit, the lights dimmed,
and all I could focus on was you,
up on the balcony, in the soft glow.

If I were an artist,
I would paint that one moment;
you, just sitting there—

a masterpiece.

Your handsome face,
your hair,
you dressed all in black...

I had never seen you look more dashing.

I'm tearing up even now,
with the memory of how awestruck I was,
gazing up at you,
knowing I already had been given
one of the best gifts in the world
in knowing you.

I try not to lavish on you as much as I used to...
but those feelings never wane.

This longing, always in my heart.

I refrain from many things I want to say,
but my darling... my heart still calls your name,
my mind still adventures always with you.

As bittersweet
as this decadence may be...
as I long for honeyed words
and milky glances
as you used to.

Time moves painfully fast,
yet achingly slow
for the anticipation that I have
that does not leave me...

I still can hold the mere magic
of those rare moments,
however few...
so intense and compact
that they still hold their power over me.

I don't wish this to ever end,
I don't wish to hide my feelings from you...
as it does nothing but torture my soul.

I had to write this letter,
because I had to clear my thoughts,
because every time I think
of Christmas Eve,
you will pop into my mind--
all awash in candlelight.

You took my breath away,
I tend to always find myself
having to remind myself to
b r e a t h e...
even now, just thinking of you.

CHRISTMAS MEMORIES

Memories of Christmas past are present in my thoughts,
the dressing up, the candlelight, the gifts that we had brought.

The garlands hung from balconies while singing filled the air.
I shuffled through the hymnal's pages, quickly, but with care.

The turkey was in the oven, with stuffing on the side,
with caroling, like "sleigh bells ring" as we'd go for a ride.

The lights had all been carefully strung on every house and tree.
Nativities were fashioned with Kings on bended knee.

Like magic, snowflakes start to fall, they dance on their way down
they land on everything in sight, blanketing the ground.

As far as thoughts, mine start to drift, much like the fallen snow
I think lovingly of family, and the friends I've grown to know.

I pray for them that Christmastime will bring them all good cheer,
and pray for health and wealth for them in the coming year.

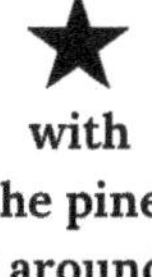

with
the pines
all around, as
if guarding me.

Frost just t r y i n g
to BITE my nose

dances

in the solitude
of night.

ABOUT THE AUTHOR

VAUGHN ROSTE

Canadian by birth, Vaughn Roste currently lives in Indiana. He is a published author of books, plays, poems, peer-reviewed articles, book reviews, program notes for CD liners and Carnegie Hall, and a doctoral dissertation. His first book, The Xenophobe's Guide to the Canadians, was published by Oval Books in England. He has two WWII films currently in pre-production, ORADOUR and THE NINE LIVES OF WALKER HARRIS. His 20-min short film FIREFIGHTER was produced by M3 Studios and is available on Youtube, and another script entitled WORST. FILM. EVER. is scheduled to be shot later in 2023 by Milepost42 Studios. His stage play, THE NAME OF THE GAME won the Leo Award for Best Overall Script at the 2021 Da Vinci International Film Festival for Best Overall Script, beating out features and shorts - the first time a play has been awarded this prize. He is represented by Jason Bellitto at Citizen Skull.

VAUGHN ROSTE

VAUGHN ROSTE

A SONNET

Whene're the worries of the day your attitude depress,
when bad news or harsh words you hear discourage and oppress;
when words meant to inspire you seem trite and so cliché:
"Chin up," "Take heart," "Be strong, my friend—today's a brand new day."

When problems all surround you but solutions are unclear,
when life still throws at you its worst but yet there's more to fear;
when unanticipated loss bereaves us of what's dear,
when day begins with no real sense of hope, or joy, or cheer;

stress threatens to engulf us, and dark mountains loom so steep,
but people tell you "just buck up" and "turn the other cheek"
and you won't let them see you cry for fear they'll think you're weak.

Remember this, and breathe, my child, for you are not alone:
your worth is not something that you should ever have to prove.
All you need to know is that you're human, and are loved.

This Christmas, I would like a moment, just one,
to have space to breathe in the quiet, alone.
Just me and the tree lights, the fireplace lit,
one moment that's all to myself to just sit.

The presents are wrapped, the shopping is done,
no concerts or pageants, no email, no phone.
One single moment to bask in the tree
that's drowning in baubles, laden with memory.

Perhaps there is joy o'er in Bethlehem town,
but here it's more solemn as Christmas slogs on.
Alone with my thoughts of just you and me,
a moment to pause, rest, cry, and just be.

A time I can ponder the year that has passed,
a moment reminds us that nothing will last.
After the children are finally asleep,
I'll probably collapse from exhaustion and weep.

Hot cocoa in hand with liqueur in it too,
I'll finally find space in my life to mourn you.
A toast I will lift as I raise up my glass
to grieve the old ghosts of my own Christmas past.

The kids will rise early, wanting their presents,
But all I want this year is your calming presence.
You had so many gifts, but no presence to give
to our family this Christmas: you no longer live.

It was never about the toys under the tree,
It was always about love, friends, and family.
I wish we had realized before you had died—
what I'd give now to have you by my side.

I'll stare as the lights shine on from the tree
and brighten the entire room save me.
Tomorrow I'll value the light they provide,
but tonight I'm consumed in the darkness they hide.

MY SOLE REQUEST

VAUGHN ROSTE

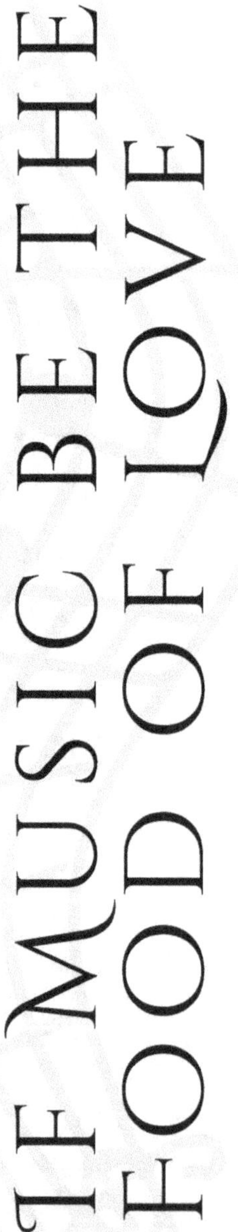

If music be the food of love then
poetry's the aperitif!
Let sonorous pitches fill our souls—
where intellect and beauty meet.

Let clever little turns of phrase
season our conversational dish.
Let profundity and wisdom spice
our entrées into relationship.

Like meals, may all our conversations be
commenced with simple grace.
May friendly words and banter
long bring smiles to a friend's face.

May gallantry and chivalry all
strengthen our rapport,
and may our faults, both large and small,
be graciously ignored.

May all our words to others leave
pleasant remembrance on our tongue,
like wine that warms our very soul—
like harmonies well sung.

And when the time comes, as it must,
that we should bid adieu,
may we find our frames refreshed
and our spirits renewed.

May the sweet sorrow of farewell
taste like a choice dessert,
like melodies that fill our souls
in harmonious concert.

The world is cold,
and bleak, and harsh.
The night is dark.
The wind is strong.

But I feel safe
here in your arms,
where I am warm,
and held, and loved.

THE WORLD IS COLD

Last Sunday, when I saw you last,
we laughed just like in days gone past.
I caught you up, we ate like kings,
you chided me for the same old things.

We parted on amicable terms
our rapport strong and reaffirmed,
but back then little did we know,
at that time, not long ago,
that that was our last Sunday.

If I knew then what I know now,
I'd never leave so soon, I vow;
I'd want to talk more, hang, and play,
but that was our last Sunday.

I hope that now, where 'ere you be,
you hold fond memories of me.
I hope that, someday soon, you smile,
remembr'ing fondly, just awhile,
the fun we had last Sunday.

If I knew then what I know now,
I'd never leave so soon, I vow;
I'd want to talk more, sing, and play,
prolonging for just one more day,
perhaps to you, my love convey,
and beg for one more Christmas day—
but that was our last Sunday.

WINTER

I refuse to wash the window
where you put your grimy hands
waiting for Daddy to come home.

I still step on your toys.
I never pick them up.
That way I can still
chastise you in my mind.

**You're still here,
yet you're not.**

Your room is as you left it,
bed unmade.
I never breach the sanctuary
for fear that someday it might lose
the smell of you.

I can spend an hour by the window
just hoping you might come home.

I'm sorry for everything I said
or did wrong.

You were loved.

I cry a lot.

I read your words in the newspaper,
even though they appear in a different order.

I don't understand how
your absence can tear apart
the fabric of my universe
yet the world around me just goes on.

I don't want to go on.

ABOUT THE AUTHOR

MICHAEL J. DENNIS

Michael is a poet and author, his first published collection of poetry, *Sonnets of Love and Life*, expresses his love of the English Sonnet.
Other poetry books: *Ferris Wheels and Candy Floss*, *Blocks of Stone and Dark Steps*, *The Colours of my Rainbow*, and *Sonnets of Love and Life 2*.
His first Novel in the *Chronicle of Achren* series '*Thanatus*' introduced Almund Penny to the world followed by three Novellas '*Drugar*' '*Werwulf*' and '*Ankou*'.

A massive history fan, he brings much historical detail to even these fantasy books (although many liberties were taken) One of the principal factors found within his poetry and writing is his love of Kent, his home county, and the exploration of historical events and places.

He loves historical fiction by Conn Iggulden, M.C. Scott, Henry Sidebottom, Madeline Miller, Berwick Coates, and Bernard Cornwell.
Reading many of these books far more times than can be seen as healthy, along with many other great storytellers and poets from Keats to Wordsworth, Shakespeare to Wilfred Owen, Vita Sackville West to Sylvia Plath.

Michael, a Man of Kent, husband, father, and grandfather often found a camera in hand wandering the downs, ancient sites, or by the seashore.

On Instagram @mikejdennis5

MICHAEL J. DENNIS

THE CHRISTMAS TREE

MICHAEL J. DENNIS

We wrapped up warm, my little girl and me.
It was her turn this year as we hunt for our tree.
Her angel face lit up you see,
at the sight of this little, LITTLE,
silent Christmas tree.

So 'little' it had trouble fitting in the car!
It was large, and the most beautiful by far!
We found you in the green wood;
I first said no, but how could I really say no?
You twisted me around your little finger so.

You said, "It will be happy to come away,
and for the holidays indoors with us to stay!"
And, "I will comfort you, little tree
because you smell so sweetly!
I will kiss your cool bark each day,
and hug you before I sleep, each night...
just as your mummy would,
and whisper gently, "don't be afraid."
I will dress you in those Christmas-time things
that sleep all the year in dark boxes!"
...
As I dream of them being taken out and allowed to
shine; those sparkling glass balls, the reindeer red,
and fairies with their fluffy threads...

"Now hold up your little arms
so you can have them to hold!
Every finger will have a sparkling light,
bright and bold!"
"Now Daddy, please turn the switch!
There won't be a single place dark or unhappy..."

Your face aglow, I smile, tears in my eyes...
Yes, my darling girl, a Christmas wish
as in my thoughts, I yearn...

For those magical times, tightly in my heart, I hold.

A kaleidoscope falls,
the colour of the rain
in prismatic beauty
of leaves as they cascade
upon my heart;
blanketed soft and deep
to mask the chilly-cold
of my winter.

The air still,
dormant amongst the trees—
whilst the forest holds its breath...
waiting... waiting... waiting.

In silence the hoar frost
settles into the void—of you.

Into my loneliness.

Memories lost to the seasons
cycling in an eternal trance.

Until I...
We return, renewed.

Spinning in this uncharted vortex
of the storm; skies brooding, dark,
foreboding, impending death
beneath life's trees.

Their arms cradled, fingers laced,
they bring sweet death, falling and spinning.

A moment of glorious colour
rests upon our hearts,
a moment of triumph amidst the grey.

The cycle will fall and rise... rise and fall,
because without sweet death—
we cannot grow.

MICHAEL J. DENNIS

WINTER'S CHILDREN

CAUDATE SONNET, SONNET 149

Come now, pluck thee from winter's rotting bowl;
dark cloaked death-withered fruits so blindly picked,
by Winter's daughter as she lets conflict—
free her wild children, race o'er grassy knoll.
Howling winter winds through the forest stole.
They whisper between tree and track afflict;
snatch ankles of those who dare tread, inflict.
Icy fingers upon branches, extol!

Hoar frost-covered crackle, this dance of death;
whilst grey skies scudding, weeping this first snow,
all creatures burrowed deep from restless, creep.
Hark! Listen, Winter's children howl their breath—
awaken long-lost wolves-call, Skadi's crow,
she speaks ice within her eyes, dare not sleep.

Silent cursing she weeps,
stirring naught, over heartless flames that smile
across her stiff lips, of such keening, vile.

A name long-forgot, wile.

For I hold my tongue in quaking fear, lest
mine she will not have, case she doth call wrest!

Whimper 'on embers, blessed—
a call from death's door of those she'd once known,
such chilling laughter, calling from the crone.
Out of the dark, atone.

Across night's chill of the first fallen snow,
no footstep had fallen o'er the barrow.

SONNET 167

MILK-FLOWER OF THE SNOW

Milk-flower of the snow, child of my tears;
whilst Mother Earth in deepest slumber slept;
through storm-tossed dreams 'til the sun appears,
there gather hopes, lengthening days that crept.

So bright reflects each rare, faint smile, now cheers;
thy home where hidden life's sweet germ was kept.
As rigid fingers shake their frosty spears—
safe in midnight's soil, how the heavens wept!

Each cold heart springs-forth life from buried joy;
slowed season's music brings a tearful glow.
Lost-rotted blossoms in winter, pale and coy,
face and breasts brushed in memories of snow.

Oh! Love soon fulfills her longing desire,
her heart entwined with sacred vestal fire.

MICHAEL J. DENNIS

NOVEMBER CHILLS

As October passes, the poets sing,
of just a few bright, prosaic days
Come! November chills, this side of the snow,
and foggy morns, of drifting haze.

A few crisp Kentish mornings,
a few abstinent eyes.
Gone the tree cloaks, their bright hues,
and here, winter's chill-like muse.

But hark! The gentle bustle of the brook,
where the birds have little to say for themselves.
Yet those beguiling fingers softly touch,
the sparkling eyes of many elves.

In this winter-song remain,
deep thoughts and gentle sentiments to share,
with the wee folk, a sunny mind,
thy winter wind will bear!

Winter's silver mantle spreads o'er the land,
covering fair nature's fine vestures brail.
I gaze out over the chill valley, bland,
as I stand and stare at that sky's sad wail;
of soulful skylarks as aloft, they soar,
on fluttering wings, airy tracks explore.

A snow-white hush save yon murmuring breeze;
its low mournful sighs, through frost-fingered trees.
Sad desolation, should Gaia appease.
Wildly, she echoes nature's charms, yet tease:
oh winter, so shrill in each blast I hear,
as o'er autumns ruin mournful, sheds a tear.

Grieve not ye mortals, o'er winter's cloaked wing,
that chills through each vale, freezes Romney's plains.
From threatening dark clouds will burst forth spring,
so gently she creeps, unbinding its chains.
Come 'freshing March, winds shall render the snow,
and cheerful green appears on the down's sough.

So welcome the May Queen! Sing for her now!
She fair-smiling, the year's bounty unfolds.
As hawthorn and elders salute, they vow,
and Phoebus Apollo disarms the cold;
once more Kentish folk venture forth, and till,
o'er Kent's verdant vales, and rich soiled hills.

Until then, my muse, in your wint'ry gloom,
bright, your heart shines, beneath dark shades of
night, 'til sweet Persephone comes forth in bloom,
she gilds the fields in spring's warm, early light;
as hoar frost benumbs the rosebud, crowned,
sad death's tuneful lyre, the dark year resounds.

AN ODE TO WINTER

ABOUT THE  AUTHOR

SHARON ANDREWS

Sharon is an English poet based in the South of England. She is married with two sons and a stepdaughter who all live away. She enjoys walking her dog and singing in a local pop choir. Her poetry explores many themes in particular the human condition.

She has 5 books available on Amazon: *Moon Writing*, *A Heart Full of Haiku*, *A Soul Full of Haiku*, *Inksomnia*, and *Life Lines*

SHARON ANDREWS

BLACK SWAN

She glides across
the winter lake;
a black vision,
starkly striking
amidst her pale family,
ruffling their feathers.

With her mysterious grace,
her neck, a question mark,
elongated against the sweep
of an ashen sky.

She navigates frigid waters,
a noble silhouette, shadows
ripple reverently in her wake.

Her albino neighbours diminish.
Head atop an S curve with an
air of cool disdain upon her
scarlet bill.

She alights smoothly, stately
wings ascend into vaporous
grey.

She is a majestically regal,
otherworldly; exotic outcast
destined for distant shores.

The lake is frozen on this winter's morn.
The palest moon rests, still there in the sky.
Coalescing with the spectacle of dawn.
The light of yonder stars doth fade and die.

No breeze disturbs the stillness of this view.
I might be all alone upon this moor.
No creature yet awake nor on the move,
a ghostly mist extends towards the tor.

The lazy sun begins to warm the air.
The light of dawn emerges 'cross the earth.
My journey leads me on I know not where,
yet fills my soul with merriment and mirth.

And then I spy him from across the land,
my husband coming for to hold my hand.

WINTER SONNET

The light is diminishing,
summer's disappearing 'round the bend.
Before next spring's arrival,
it's time for things to end.

The trees will soon strip bare,
their essence hurtling to the ground.
We've lost the joy of sunshine,
but earthier things we've found.

Can you smell the rotting fruit?
This dampness will soon turn to frost.
Memories of golden cornfields,
all but forever lost.

The birds are seeking sustenance,
pecking at the frigid earth.
They are taking stock for winter,
dreaming of rebirth.

Don't lament the loss, love—
a surge is on the horizon.
Despite the naked branches,
our skin absorbs the fading sun.

A JANUARY DOG WALK

There's a chill wind a-blowing
'Cross these wetlands, and I
welcome the sting of cold.

Jack has sharpened his teeth and
bites my blushing cheeks.

A yellow-tinged, grey
blankets sparse fields.

Dog-walkers nod as they rush on—
heads down, scarves pulled tight,
dreaming of hot mugs cupped in
numb fingers.

The sun is resting in his bed, too
lazy to warm this January frost.

The placid lake scarcely ripples,
graced by neither duck nor goose.

My pup and I skate along the
boardwalk, our hearts beating in
vigorous union.

SHARON ANDREWS

REJOICE

Seems like every year there's another gap;
an empty space at the Christmas table.
Years past, we sat on Santa's lap,
now we are no longer able.

Now that we are older
there's no magic in the air.
The winter seems much colder.
Goodwill is all too rare.

We've all turned into Ebeneezer!
We're as green as Mister Grinch!
Santa is just some old geezer!
Christmas carols make us flinch!

We're all stressed with ordering gifts,
our bank manager is feeling sick.
Another year—another family rift,
no more room for Old Saint Nick.

We used to be full of charity,
ready to help our neighbours;
now we don't garland the tree,
and making friends is out of favour.

We used to deck the halls with holly;
mistletoe encouraged a kiss—
once upon a time, we were jolly,
those days so full of bliss

We sang "Do They Know it's Christmas Time"
now I wonder if we've forgot...
and it truly is a terrible crime
these days, we all feel lost.

It seems we've forgotten the reason!
We've lost our thankful voice.
Come, let's embrace the season!
It's time for us to rejoice!

CHRISTMAS WISH

My fondest Christmas wish
is this:

A simple prayer for harmony.
Sat round the table with family.

Hearts overflowing with warmth and cheer.
Keeping our loved ones ever near.

Lights reflected in smiling eyes.
Hearty carol singing, contented sighs.

A crackling fire, a dog on my lap.
Everyone having an afternoon nap.

My fondest Christmas wish
is this:

Memories of loved ones long departed.
Reliving old times so full-hearted.

Thinking of dad in his Santa suit;
with a jolly beard and shiny black boots.

Auntie Joan having a laugh.
Granny Ivy acting so daft.

Looking at old photos, all aglow.
Smiling at times we used to know.

Oh yes, my fondest Christmas wish—
is this.

ABOUT THE  AUTHOR

DOUGLAS K. CURRIER

Douglas K Currier holds a Master of Fine Arts degree from the University of Pittsburgh and has published work in a number of anthologies: Onion River: Six Vermont Poets, Getting Old, and Welcome to the Neighborhood, and journals: "Café Review," "Main Street Rag," "Comstock Review" as well as many others, both in the United States and in South America. His chapbook "Senorita Death" was recently published by Main Street Rag Publishing Company. He lives with his wife in Winooski, Vermont. His two previous collections: "Vida prestada" and "Regreso" were published in Argentina.

DOUGLAS K. CURRIER

DOUGLAS K. CURRIER

PETRARCHAN SONNET

CHRISTMAS FOR THE OLD

We don't put up a family Christmas tree,
old ornaments collect in one big box—
the strings of lights, the balls the season mocks
for lack of children young enough for glee.

The sense of wonder seasonal we see
in lights of neighbors on surrounding blocks,
and now my wife and I put up no socks,
and save the Christmas cookies for our tea.

And yet, we miss the children and the day,
excitement of the morning with the gifts,
the moments of surprise in children's eyes,

ensuing hours when the children play—
as smells of dinner set the room adrift.
Those moments we have had and now put by.

Tired of technology, he'd welcome
a little myrrh or frankincense.
Opting for the olfactory-odor
spiritual in nature—that which could
perhaps reach the nose of God.

Gold, as many problems as technology—
price fluctuating like the market, hard
to store safely, and good only for its color.

He'd ask for an additional year or two,
a bag of better memories—more vivid,
not broken like Christmas cookies.
Contrary to what his mother always said,
they don't taste the same.

He'd like to run again, perhaps play in snow,
survive a snowball fight with the shortish,
neighborhood toughs: five-year-olds,
granddaughters, and such.

Candy, he'd like candy—peach blossoms
and cordial cherries—his mother's favorite sweets.
Fruit cake with no allergic nuts, just candied fruit—
elusive as incense—reaching God's palate.

CHRISTMAS GIFTS

DOUGLAS K. CURRIER

A CHRISTMAS POEM

PETRARCHAN SONNET

The rush, the grip of the world, the tricks time plays
in pushing, pulling every day to night.
And memory does not fade, but crumbles. Slight
tears in fabric, unused, its color grays.

I like to think in these, the holidays—
perhaps a bit of ribbon, color bright,
(though nothing really makes this distance right)
that I be there in small, sequential ways.

So this small note, this need will need suffice,
these words find place, belong, beneath your tree,
these thoughts with warmth and cheer your days imbue

(lines intimate amid the snow and ice).
For just as these might cause you think of me,
I am as warmly remembering you.

What can I tell you?
It was the night
of the Cold Moon,
December shrinking,
a helium balloon
caught in a tree.
What was ending?
What beginning?
It's easy to lose track
when it's the same moon,
the same night, the same
balloon-trap tree.

What can I say?
I went out in my slippers,
the night, a shadow
dodging porch lights,
streetlamps, halogen.
What was the time?
Easy to lose track when
the minute you just lived looks
mostly like the minute ahead.

What was I waiting for?
The moon to blink its single
eye, or even a wink,
a nod, a sign—the human
need to name the same celestial
body numbers of times.

THIS EVENING

And if this is it, this evening all.
I watch the night fall as if it were the last.
A warm winter's evening
in the subtropics, look how far
I am from home—this escape, this parlor magic,
this sleight of hand, mirrors, and distance.

Will she recognize me, finally come
to settle accounts, punch the ticket
I've been holding for so many years?

What does it mean to be ready
when every glance over my shoulder,
expecting her to walk by like that girl
in the sleeveless, striped shirt—
tells me I'm not.

SIESTA IN WINTER

After the winter siesta the day

comes slowly back to life,

a small animal startled

from a cold sleep. Cold

is relative, and as such goes

where it likes—slams the doors,

checks the fridge, opens

a window, and takes

the most comfortable chair.

In these houses without heat,

it's hard to drive out, burrows

under blankets at night searching

for feet and other such extremities.

DOUGLAS K. CURRIER

DEATH IN AUTUMN

Leaves die well here. The color

is agonizing, beautiful, before the wind

takes them to fire and mulch.

Death knows that "harvest" is one

of those euphemisms used

to slight her the credit she deserves.

Here, plants; useful or prickly,

handsome or plain, die—call it

what you will. Animals stay busy

and out of death's way—while the old folk,

begin to think perhaps, to make it

through another winter. You might

see her, a schoolgirl perhaps,

striding along, kicking drifts of leaves,

wind licking her sear dress of leaves.

Born in the cold womb of winter,
(well after holidays, rejoicing and light,
drifting snow), I am the cusp of spring;
the sodden, brown crust of snow-turned-ice—
a freezer burn that renders the frozen, useless.

February has no redemption, no redeeming
qualities; except its oddness and brevity,
(deserves little notice), an uncertain filler—
an afterthought—a mistake made
to make an even dozen.

Hard-candy heart in the middle—little
warmth. Another opportunity for love to fail—
again—in an orgy of ostentation, expectation,
and waste... chocolate, flowers, stuffed animals
take center stage, and even Cupid blushes.

FEBRUARY

About the Author

Ann Marie Eleazer

Ann Marie Eleazer, author of *She's Magic & Midnight Lace* and *The Girl With Salem In Her Eyes* has always considered herself to be a bit ancient, haunted and otherworldly. She is someone who enjoys enchanted flights through the dark fairytales and magical places she's been drawn to since childhood.

facebook.com/shesmagicandmidnightlace

Instagram.com/shesmagicandmidnightlace_

getbook.at/SMML
mybook.to/salem

ANN MARIE ELEAZER

ANN MARIE ELEAZER

She's the raven
casting jingle spells,
and he's the
dark winter's night
promising her
a cold moon.

It's a promise
she's always wanted,
but never dared to dream.

He calls to her
on Christmas Eve
upon her black
and magical wings.

And with a chilly grip,
he dances her
to the midnight stars.

Peaceful, mirthy,
and all that's true,
forever in his arms.

The way she works her magic,
turning men into poetry,
and her thoughts
into howling wings...

Blackened wild,
beautifully dressed
in "'tis the season" to be
joyfully unhinged.

But beware
the woman who has
her mysteries figured out!

Her hunger
knows no bounds.

She leaves the wolves
quite needy
as they scream and shout, and pout.

ANN MARIE ELEAZER

LADY FROST

Can you hear the way
she howls your name
in the winter's wind?

Lady Frost is at it again:
with dark cranberry lips,
mistletoe hips,
and a touch of snowy magic.

Her locks of coal will come
sip on your soul—
until the glow of spring
returns from her den.

Everything about her
wept darkness...
her tales of woe,
her eyes,
her love of winter dusk,
and silky black holiday dresses.

If you're looking for her
this Christmas,
she will be falling in love
within an old Dickens' tale,
creeping through
dark forests of pine—
looking for the perfect tree,
or nestled by the fire,
with stockings full of spells
and a cup of fairy tea.

HER TALES OF WOE

ABOUT THE AUTHOR

MARIA THÉRÈSE WILLIAMS

Maria Thérèse Williams has lived her whole life in the county of Kent, England. She is the author of the *Roaming Reflections* collections, all available on Amazon. She loves creative expression, being as comfortable with physical choreography as literary choreography.

She is married with three grown-up children and her family is her greatest treasure. A close second was her community dance school which she created and ran for 12 years until retiring in 2016.

As well as her 30 years as a teacher of dance, Maria has garnered a wide range of other professional experiences, including Human Resources across banking and retail and support working in the NHS for departments such as Learning Disabilities, Dementia Support, and Cancer Services.

Her poetry and prose feature in anthologies such as *Absolutely Poetry* produced by Wheelsong Books, and *Shadows of the Past are Wings of Future*. She has been featured in *Open Door Magazine* and can often be heard on BBC Radio Kent's *Upload* program. Her work "Nurture Nature" features throughout the documentary film "*When the Rare Orchid Blooms*" by Film Café Co-op.

She loves all art but ultimately, loves to read, write and dance. Her muse is life, itself, inspired by psychology, spirituality, nature, relationships, and all the many aspects of existence in this universe.

You can find her poetry and prose on:

Instagram at https://Instagram.com/@roaming_reflections

Facebook Page at www.facebook.com/RoamingReflections

or hear some of them at her

YouTube channel at Roaming Reflections - YouTube

- SAMHAIN
- SAMHAIN SCENE
- AUTUMN GRACE
- WINTER WALK
- THE LONGEST NIGHT
- WARMTH OF CHRISTMAS PAST
- TETRAD OF TREATS
- SPIRIT OF CHRISTMAS
- CRIMBO GLOW
- FIRESIDE FESTIVAL
- OLD HALLOWMAS EVE

MARIA THÉRÈSE WILLIAMS

Bringing in **All Saints Day**
from the sunset of **Halloween**;
is the arrival of our winter,
the pagan festival of **Samhain.**

The costumes and the bonfires,
the spirits and the ghouls—
may wrongly trick you into thinking
these treats are one and all!

Our harvest is completed,
and we prepare the food to keep,
as we protect ourselves from angry ghosts
who may join us as we sleep.

The darker nights are winter's gift
until the sun returns, reborn;
and a thinning veil welcomes
friendly spirits to our realm.

We remember all our loved ones,
ancestors to be heard,
and make offerings to gods in return
for protection for our world.

Bonfires cleanse the old year
and protect the year to come—
The **Wheel of Life** reflected
with costumes, dance and song.

These costumes keep us hidden
from the spirits who mean ill,
As we hope the god of the dark time
will permit our healing spells.

So fairies, spirits, come do your mischief,
we welcome your sense of fun!
If you mean us no harm you can join us
in the comfort of our home.

We'll leave you out some sustenance,
or perhaps, a glass of wine.
It's respect and honour we offer you,
at this transitional time.

As the supernatural and human worlds
embrace a moment to join,
non-human forces may be just what
we need to make Earth shine.

Creation needs compassion,
but these times seem 'specially dark,
the **Day of the Dead** should be a time
we listen while they speak!

As we dry herbs and burn incense
and reflect on all our faults,
may our visitors show us how to repent
for our nefarious deeds;
we have neglected nature;
been enemy of all things good.
Remnants of pagan gods & nature's spirits—
join us in our dance;
so we chant of life and death,
deeply feeling for our chance—
to renew our love and harmony
in all things good and natural;
a wheel around the bonfire,
demonstrating our remonstrance,
reconciling and celebrating ALL realms
in the hope to save our souls.

MARIA THÉRÈSE WILLIAMS

SAMHAIN SCENE

Through a gossamer veil of delicate tangerine,
ghosts of our ancestors can vaguely be seen.
They bestow their presence in this realm,
at the close of every autumn.

Guardians of creation await our humble offerings,
as we garner fruits from the conclusion of the harvest;
and we ignite fires to cleanse the old year
embracing the approaching winter.

Only on this spice-tinged anniversary
do we indulge our belief
that all our precious souls are unceasing.
Witchcraft endeavours to hinder those evil,
while we welcome our loved ones home.

Our deepest tales of life and death are expressed
in costumed dances around the cleansing fires.
Examining our consciences, hoping we've met,
and indulged in our creation's gods desires.

AUTUMN GRACE

My love, right now,
wears autumn hues,
vibrations of nature,
and all that's true.

It swells from the songs
sung by the trees—
to which the leaves
dance on the breeze.

My soul soars high,
my heart grows strong,
from a rich, golden sense
of where I belong.

This wonderful, magical,
woodland space—
where autumn leaves circle
with spiritual grace.

MARIA THÉRÈSE WILLIAMS

WINTER WALK

With muffled tread on a deep, winter carpet—
every step feels therapy of effort.

All of the trees in crystal gowns,
the clear air amplifies nature's sounds.

The bright, the white of this winter vision,
brings gladness to my morning mission.

Guiding my thinking through bird-song and trees,
I get to come home with my mind at ease.

THE LONGEST NIGHT

Never before has the return of the sun
been so desired!
Flame the Yule Log, and bask twelve days
in the light of its fire!

Hang evergreens and mistletoe
above every door—
in hope for more goodwill
than ever before.

Our sun pauses for a moment,
on top of the world...
Midwinter's upon us
and we welcome her rebirth.

It seems this winter has been *two years*
in our presence,
we beg relief; we beg for light, do we
need forgiveness?

The birth of the Son
is celebrated soon,
may the blessing of His light,
the stars, sun, and moon—

destroy this darkness
which has engulfed us so long—
and bring freedom to our spirits,
a song of light for our soul.

MARIA THÉRÈSE WILLIAMS

WARMTH OF CHRISTMAS PAST

Three pairs of eyes that won't go to sleep,
so that we can give Santa the all-clear to creep—
into their rooms with stockings of toys,
before surrounding the tree with even more joys!

We've left out the whisky, mince pie, and a carrot,
and repeat the instructions just like a parrot;
"Santa won't come until you're all asleep!"
and "His elves will tell him if you take a peek!"

But the excitement is tangible all through the night,
and we can't help but smile (try as we might)
at all the excuses our little ones make—
as to why they have reasons to stay wide awake.

So Santa steers clear until half past three,
our eyelids so low, we hardly can see...
Finally, we snuggle up into our beds,
but in half an hour, three little heads—
are peeking around our bedroom door.

We watch their unwrapping, their eyes wide in awe.
How can we moan at our lack of rest, when we're
painfully aware of how quickly this will pass?

We take them downstairs, and they wait at the door
(they're hoping that Santa has left them much more!)
You can't see the carpet, for all of the presents,
and the looks on their faces, are as good as it gets.

Christmas is magical, the atmosphere's bright—
with love and the laughter of our children's delight.
In a blink of an eye, they're all fully grown,
so we warm in the memories
of the Christmases, we've known

TETRAD OF TREATS

Your gift of **love** brings with it, trust,
and the desire to offer protection.

Your gift of **strength** brings with it, faith
and life's necessary determination.

Your gift of **courage** maintains your hopes
and your brave heart full of confidence.

Your gift of **grace** honours you for your
bestowing compassion and forgiveness.

MARIA THÉRÈSE WILLIAMS

SPIRIT OF CHRISTMAS

Spirit of Christmas, I need no things, instead— I give thanks for splendid beings; times this year, they have helped me so much— so wrap them in comfort and a lifetime of love.

CRIMBO GLOW

A jolly little man in a bright red suit,
tiny little fairies and elves, so cute!

Brighten up our lives with the promise of new light—
which illuminated the reindeer steering Santa's flight.

Dancing around in children's dreams—
are gingerbread men and candy canes.

Flying high, amongst the sparkling stars,
past the man in the moon who guards our hearts;

which feel they'll burst in the expectation,
of wishes granted and the world's salvation,

As a new year is welcomed and gifts are bestowed
on family and friends who make our lives glow.

FIRESIDE FESTIVAL

The world gently fades through my lashes,
and a herd of decorated reindeer dashes—
across the velvet sky up high;
causing the clouds to sprinkle snowflakes,
which pirouette through the air.
And I can only stare—
at the jolly old man dressed up, nice and warm—
not just in his suit, but in the world's anticipation.
The hope and excitement of not just our children,
enchanted by tales of generosity.
Our eyes wide in expectation,
glowing in the new light brought into being;
the solstice and the Son, both thrilling.
Rewarding our wait by granting our wishes
by filling our faith with festive miracles.
Fairies and elves dance around the open fire,
singing and laughing in the warmth of love.
Mistletoe kisses and chilly snow angels,
feasting on candy and sipping on icicles.
Lost in a wonderland of belief in Santa Claus,
their jobs in the workshop on pause for a day;
to make way for rejoicing in this Yuletide festivity.
Soaking up the atmosphere like the scent of pine cones,
embracing the promise of a better future
proclaimed by the angels.
And through the vapours above the cosy log fire—
the spirit of a newborn baby, cradled by Santa.
A new star, a new sun, and happiness for everyone!
It seems my dreams are no stranger
to the contemplation of every nation.
Looking up, looking forward—
as the birth of Jesus ameliorates our future.

OLD HALLOWMAS EVE

The wind howled and the snow swirled around
in a perishing storm of new winter,
when a man and his horse, barely holding their course
came across a poor, shivering beggar.
Having only his cloak between him and the cold,
compassion struck him in a compelling hold.
He grabbed his mighty sword, sharp and true,
slicing his military cloak clean in two.
Each half would ensure that both men could endure
at least some of this icy cold weather.

That night the man dreamed of his generous deed,
but the figure he'd wrapped was no beggar—
but Christ, himself donned the half cloak,
and addressed His angels with vigor;
"Here is Martin, the Roman soldier,
whom I have just baptized. He has clothed me!"
And as recorded in St Matthew's line;
"Whatsoever you do to the least of my brothers,
"so, you do unto me."
The pagan soldier had been blessed into Christianity,
Martin became a Bishop of Gaul.
His little cape becoming a legend.
The Cappella, overseen by who we now call chaplains,
would be a holy relic forever.

His Feast day is set on his funeral date,
which falls on 11th November;
when children parade with lanterns they've made
Singing Martin songs at each door—
where they're gifted with sweets or similar treats
on this Old Hallowmas Eve.

Latin "Cappella" means Little Cape
"Cappellini" now means Chaplain
"Cappella" now means Chapel
Chapel means private sanctuary or holy place
In music, "a cappella" means "in the manner of a chapel", becoming "church music written to
accompany voices in religious services" which has now come to mean "unaccompanied vocal
music"
"Old Halloween" marked the end of the harvest and the beginning of winter but also
"Saint Martin's Lent", the 40 days to the Epiphany.

ABOUT THE  AUTHOR

TOMÁS J. COLÓN

Tomás has always found poetry to be the one safe place to freely express everything that has moved him in his journey through life. He believes self-reflection and purposeful introspection to be some of the most valuable tools we have at our disposal to become our better selves. He shares his journey through poetry with the hopes of reaching out to others who may struggle while feeling that they are alone in their troubles. Tomás firmly believes that poetry is the collective voice of the human experience and that thought is what fuels him to express himself through this art form.

When prodded a bit to tell us a little more about himself, this is what he said; "I am an Army Veteran of 12 years and father of 4 amazing children, three of which are actively serving in the military currently. My wife and I have been married for 26 years. My daughter is living with us and makes us feel old like she has to take care of us or something, but we just disappear without a trace on the weekends... I guess that makes her kinda nervous, but my wife and I think it's hilarious! I grew up the product of the absent father phenomenon, as my dad left when I was 3 and never came back. I am a social worker in the field of child protective investigations where I supervise a specialized unit. I LOVE CIGARS AND BOURBON!!!! And I'm an ambivert who seeks moments of silence and deep introspection...... ohhhh, ohhh and I am a Libra and I love long walks on the beach..."

Instagram @thoughts2verses

Several books available on Amazon, check out bio on Instagram.

GELID HANDS

SWAYING SPANISH MOSS

DETACHED

BLUE

FORGOT ABOUT THE SUN

CANVAS

HAMILTON PARK

TOMÁS J. COLÓN 

GELID HANDS

Faintly audible rhythm,
like muffled Afro-Cuban percussion;
beating, retreating
beating, beating,
beating, and retreating...
Seeking, digging,
desperately carving its way
through these hiemal rivers
flowing through my chest.

Through these arteries
that somehow remain—
an unmapped autobahn of hope;
An internal highway where
love and memories
once traveled unrestrained.

I meandered one night
in the world of dreams,
the journey led me to
a field of flickering stars—
I turned and gazed quietly upon
this world of wandering wonders.

I saw the fragile beauty of this Earth,
realizing that it was being
gently caressed by
a hyperborean hand—I
wrestled it away,
pressed it firmly against my chest—
wanting to give it all
the warmth of my heart.

WINTER

Oblivious of the impending outcome,
I awakened—
finding myself in this wintry cage,
shaking from
the shrewd temperatures
of despair:
gelid hands pinning me down.

The frigid tundra of broken promises,
patiently waiting for proof of life—
Listening intently
to faintly audible rhythms
of the muffled Afro-Cuban percussion;
praying it would resume its arduous fight...

Beating, retreating
beating, beating,
beating and retreating.

Seeking, digging,
carving its way, desperately,
through these hiemal rivers
flowing through my chest...

SWAYING SPANISH MOSS

The sun sets
behind inconspicuous hues of
powder blue skies,
bone white clouds,
quiet shades of
nocturnal transition
seeping through—
creating apricot patches
on heaven's lower canvas; as
I contemplate the
undeterred majesty of time.

Recognizing I am but
a grain of sand traveling about
the Spanish moss;
descending from live oak trees—
swaying ever so gently in
the evening breeze.

I close my tired eyes,
simply because the
curious child that
dwells within me became
quite restless—
wanting to appreciate
visions that only the soul can see.
It always seems to
awaken the inner me...
it is only then that
the image of
the grand universal clock is clearest.
It is there, where to
the most lucid understanding
of my mortality,
I am nearest.

WINTER

But again my
memory sways
like the Spanish moss
from live oak trees—
ever so gently, as if
my mind itself was
lovingly cradled by
these evening winds—
and I wondered;

I wondered if... (before I
lay to sleep tonight)
if my last words to
everyone I love,
were words that would
make their hearts smile—
if I could not find my way back
from these visions that
only the souls can see as
the sun sets;
behind inconspicuous hues of
powder blue skies,
bone white clouds,
quiet shades of
nocturnal transition
seeping through,
creating apricot patches
on heaven's lower canvas; as
I contemplate the
undeterred majesty of time;
recognizing I am but
a grain of sand traveling about...

TOMÁS J. COLÓN

Untethered from this realm,
I unplugged myself,
again—
keeping my existence
silently tucked away...
hidden in a sealed graphene box.

My senses paused,
and I ask my creator;
Is this a gift?
Did you intend for me to feel—everything?"

I feel empty at times—missing
the laughter of my children.
I feel lost at times—wondering where it is
this journey is going to lead...

Is this a gift?—this necessity to let this pen bleed,
to find words and phrases to
describe these emotions, these experiences?

What if I am simply overwhelmed?

For I have pleaded with my creator;
the answers have not been many;

If this is a gift,
I pray you would allow me to detach—
that you would
allow me to know what it is to
not feel, not care!

A moment to live free of anxiety.

Allow me to walk in serenity—
to not be consumed with always
fleeing from the grips of depression.

I am weary;
tired of isolating myself and
smiling,
as if this world
made me feel as if
this journey of mine was
a worthwhile venture.

My knees ache.
These hands have lost strength and
can barely maintain their proximity.

In my moments of prayer,
trapped in this sealed
graphene box,
I desperately try to find light
in this vantablack existence.
So I have
untethered from this realm,
unplugged myself, again;
asking my creator,
"Is this a gift?
Did you intend for me to feel—everything?"

Solace is an attentive paramour
for she has always been there;
there at every turn when
healing required a quiet space,
an uninterrupted place.

She has gifted me with soothing sounds,
rendered everything silent unto jazz.
Everything except my deepest thoughts—
those thoughts danced effortlessly
in tandem with old brass horns and
ebony and ivory keys.

The entire room, awash in indigo sadness,
leaving only the warm amber hue
of a smoky Kentucky Bourbon
neatly resting in my glass.
This preoccupied mind of mine
running aimlessly through
a legion of cerulean-tinged "what ifs."
Wondering "what if I
could simply let go—
to let myself be immersed in
the oceans of your
Neptune soul?"

BLUE

"What if our love
found an untimely demise?"
"What if I am not strong enough?"
"What if my universe could not contain
a love like two colliding galaxies?"
"A love with a cyan glow that rivals
the birth of a star?"
"What if azure angels are late
to carry my cobalt prayers
to heavens gate?"

I can *feel* blue.
Today blue is tangible.
Blue became the swaying bridge
between the tingling sensation of hope
and the asphyxiation of
feeling despondent.

Today blue feels like questions.
Today blue feels like
the absence of answers.
Today blue feels merciful enough
to let me still see
the warm amber hue
of this Kentucky bourbon....

TOMÁS J. COLÓN

FORGOT ABOUT THE SUN

One day I
unwittingly forgot
about the sun.

My world became
endless firs blanketed in
virgin snow—
soaring pine trees
majestically draped in
legions of resting snowflakes.

And she held me,
just as I was aimlessly running
toward the summer.

Love became;
a lingering winter,
a subtle scent of cocoa,
a warm blanket,
gentle whispers—
promising me
all the warmth
the sun could never
reach me with.

Her soul took hold of me,
refusing to leave.
My world became
endless firs blanketed in
virgin snow,
soaring pine trees
draped in resting snowflakes,
quiet and pure,
still and gentle;
a love as persistent as
a lingering winter.

That one day,
she unexpectedly
became my sun...

CANVAS

With wonderful colors
we paint the canvas
that is life.
Graceful, every brush stroke
as it brings forth
beauty for all to see.
Looks of admiration
without any hint
of what lies beneath.

The splendid array of colors,
hidden
beneath the surface;
behind the tranquility
that is projected
on this canvas.

Troubled waters
of unknown oceans
violently crash against
the walls of a fractured heart.
We are careful to
paint an image
which will cover every inch
leaving not a single
space from which
pain can escape.

With wonderful colors
we paint the canvas
that is life.
Masterful is every brush stroke,
what artistry lies in us all...

HAMILTON PARK

Passions burn deep within;
a furnace fueled by
shattered dreams and
unanswered prayers—simply
wanting to be the one who made it.

Black boots, unlaced.
Baggy black jeans.
Black hood over the
headphones through which-
I tuned out the world.

Walking through
brick buildings.
Hopes, frozen in time;
cold air finds me
on every dark corner.

Just after midnight-
Hamilton Park, dimly lit,
on a cold stone seat
looking at a stone chess table
absent all its pieces.

The strategy always
seems to be survival.
Even on this "level" playing field,
I'm always two moves behind
without ever gaining the advantage.

WINTER

I bang my fist upon
this stone table;
tears descend from my
disillusioned eyes and onto
my cold angry face.

Black boots, unlaced.
Baggy black jeans.
Black hood over the
headphones through which-
I tuned out the world.

I brave the cold winds
looking for the light.
Enveloped by a darkness
that befriends only he
who abandons all hope.

That stone chess table in
dimly lit Hamilton Park—
my confession booth.
With no one around I cried,
hoping to be the one who made it...

ABOUT THE  AUTHOR

P'TRISHA W. CHANEY

The first poem Trish remembers writing was a tribute to one of her Wolf-Hybrid dogs that had just passed away. "I was completely devastated," she said, "as my family and I had raised her and her brother from pups 12 weeks to 14-15 years old."

"It was also a time in my life when many things were changing - job, relationships, livelihood, and residence. And, most times, I've found, as hard as it is, you have to let go of things, to allow room for new ... experiences, places, and people to take their place. So, the poem served as a comfort ... and release."

Trish majored in Theatre Arts at Virginia Tech, then moved to California when her husband got a job in Silicon Valley. She had to coordinate a lot of "left brain, right brain" activities, because, even though one of her day jobs at Apple Computer was as a project manager, she was still participating in theatre projects and musical endeavors in the evenings. While at Apple, her teammates in the Instructional Products division discovered her "reading voice, " which started her voice-over career instructing new computer users how to turn on the Macintosh and use the mouse!

Trish describes her style as "quirky and whimsical, and I like to rhyme. Don't know why, it just comes to me that way. I performed in many Shakespeare festivals (every summer in California), so I have iambic pentameter and trochaic speech patterns embedded in my soul. Plus, with all the singing I do, it just seems to flow out of me that way."

Here's to life that is ever-changing. I hope you enjoy.

P'TRISHA W. CHANEY

P'TRISHA W. CHANEY

MAKITA CHEWBACCA LITTLEBEAR

I went to see the Old One, a Wolf I'd always known,
He lived up in the Mountains, the place I once called Home.

We'd play, when we were younger, and run amongst the trees,
and howl with Laughter on the wind, then fall upon our knees.
We'd dig the Earth together, looking for great treasure,
a mole for him ... perhaps gold for me? whatever gave us pleasure.

And when the day was done, we'd sit on Mountaintop
and glory in the colored sky as the Sun began its drop.
He'd place his paw upon my hand, together we would stay,
and think about our lives entwined, and how we got that way.

———————————

So, here I was again, many Moons beyond,
and there he was ... an older Wolf ... of whom I am so fond.
I didn't think he'd know me, or remember who I was,
but then he lifted his old head and stretched out both his paws.

He seemed a little blinded now, his hearing not so great,
but he could smell, and feel my Heart, and how it really ached.
He got up to meet me ... and that was no small feat ...
for him to rise and stand ... was such an honored treat.

84

WINTER

I kissed his muzzle, now so soft, and ruffled up his mane,
for he was "my little lion" in many of our games.
We walked for just a little, 'til he could stand no more,
and then we sat, both on the ground, just outside the door.

I told him how my life had been, and how I missed him so,
and ... that if he needed ... he could surely ... go.
I told him that I loved him, and ... that ... he did concur,
And then I buried my tearful face into his thickened fur.

He placed his paw upon my hand and I remembered what that meant.
... that he is always with me, no matter where our Time is spent.

P'TRISHA W. CHANEY

JANUARY, THE WOLF MOON

Come close to me
in your perigee,
Let us dance and howl
with laughter.

With Mars to your left,
leave no soul bereft
of your luminous beauty
and rapture.

I watch you arise,
very large in the sky
an illusion perhaps of the distance.

No matter how far
or distant you are,
To me, you consume all the instance.

IN THE EARLY MORNING SNOW

Kitty footprints in the snow
lead to places that I know.
One stops here at Catnip Pot
to see if any herb it's got.

Once refreshed by nosing 'round,
the steps lead forward, this I found ...
through the carport, under car,
well, he doesn't go too far.

He doubles back against the tree.
Wonder what his mission be?
Checking here and there ... what's this?
Another set of paws I missed??

Black of cat and white of snow
makes no difference in the toe.
except where there are six, you see
five for him, but six there be.

Ahh, that's Momma Hemingway,
don't know how she got that way,
but, in showshoe, she defends
and seems to get the upper ... hand.

A playful game here thus ensued
between them both of fur and 'tude.

Quiet, peaceful snow at night
becomes a treasured map, daylight.

THE HAINT: AN ACTOR'S EPITAPH

Some day ... as I grow older,
I want to be ... a ghost!
and sail along with legless movement,
hovering coast to coast.

I'd be a friendly happenstance!
... a willing confidant ...
to those who'd take the chance to know me
why, even those who'd say they ... "can't!"

And you wouldn't even know t'was me
that tickled at your chin,
just think of all the fun I'd have
... or the trouble you'd be in!

Then I would ne'er be lonely!
(Well, it's not that I am now;
but it would beat the possibility
of returning as a ... cow!)

Yet, if you say we don't return,
why, what a pickle I'd be in
trapped forever 'neath the dirt
with no way to make amends?

So, let my Spirit soar,
and let me practice ... here
to reach your Spirits, in this life
and give you wondrous cheer.

For I want to make you laugh!
I ... long ... to make you cry.
I want to ... touch you ... in some way,
before I say,
... goodbye.

THOUGHTS

89

It is said the Energy we possess,

will surpass our Time on Earth,

that Gravity will release us,

no matter what our worth.

And all our Calculations

concerning Math and Space,

will have no bearing on Destination

when we leave this place.

About the Author

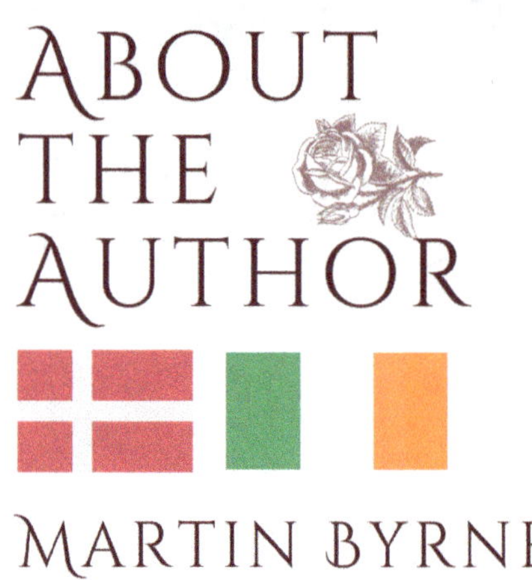

MARTIN BYRNE

Martin Byrne was born and raised in Liverpool, England. Graduating from school, he embarked on many and varied careers, including mechanical engineering, hospitality, and transportation. His love of reading adventure stories as a child, also fueled his desire to travel. Currently resident in Denmark, he has two boys with his ex-wife. Although writing poetry is a hobby for him, he draws inspiration from his life experiences as well as the beauty of nature that surrounds the small seaside town where he lives.

Magazine publications: one piece in *Unicorn Magazine*, Vol No.6, December 2021.

Anthology: three pieces, one in each volume of *Unchaining Freedom Trilogy* (Our Earthians Community Group), Ink Gladiator Press 2022.

MARTIN BYRNE

WINTER KISSED DREAMS

Autumn bade the last goodbye
before the charge of Eyvindr.
A sharp breath from the frigid North
and colder than a frostbit morn.

Decaying leaves crack underfoot
as we traverse the sleepy wood.
Branches stripped, naked and bare,
creak and bend in the violent gust
vainly grasping marble clouds
that hide an incandescent sky.

As giant flakes begin to fall
and melt upon our glowing skin;
winter's kiss, most beguiling
hastens the tempest to begin.

Winter! Savage and relentless!
Streams transform to frosted glass
and the earth to cold-pressed steel.
Huddled around, roaring hearths
adorned by boughs of evergreen
we watch intently, the gentle fall.

A deep calm settles upon the land
the night reflects, crystals dazzling
and snug beneath this virgin blanket
Freyja sleeps, and dreams of spring.

AUTUMN'S CANVAS

Yesterday felt, like an age ago;
when fingers coolly swept my hair,
the fiery sun; freckling skin,
cascading waves; filling the air.
This spinning Earth, orbiting
that lonely star we call Sun.
Sipping the last of summer's wine
in awe of the setting horizon.

Bowing trees, with dappled leaves
subliminally turn sanguine.
A camouflage or earthy blend?
My senses rise, to overcome.
A mischievous breeze catches,
drifting leaves that pirouette.
Nature's ballet gracefully plays
an enchantment for all to see.

Mourn? Not I - summer's demise,
her gifts comprise, more than just life;
poetry, and art, through vivid
palettes, of autumn's russet light.

SUNDAY MORNING

The cup of coffee warms my hand
and the ponderous swirl of cream,
contrasts the racing grey outside,
hissing, whistling past the window,
casting the cold and heavy rain
on the cavernous street below.

A hunched figure, struggles forward
clutching brolly and plastic bag,
that flaps, twists in the icy blast
propelling leaves and paper scraps,
that loop and dip and somersault
along an invisible track.

Then you're here in our apartment
dripping brolly and plastic bag.
Bedraggled and frozen, you beam
a smile and show me what you've got:
New York bagels, eggs, and cream cheese
from our local grocery shop.

We sit together, warm, and snug
watching the tempest rage outside
contrast our brunch of scrambled eggs,
toasted bagels with sticky cheese
and sip a hot cup of coffee,
laced with a swirl of double cream.

VEILED

The drapes are drawn in the back of my mind,
mourning the passage of autumn's burnt gold.
Memories linger like leaves on the beech,
alone on the cusp of winter's deep frost.
Recalling light days and breezy cool nights,
sweeping and lifting your soft auburn crown.
The mirth in your songs, your voice on the wind,
a kiss: redolent like pearly dew rain.

Rooted in earth, the mountain is lonely,
watching the firmament slowly decline.
Oceans revealing a shipwreck of dreams,
fallow words turning to dust in my mouth.
Yet I know not, what silence was before:
nor cannot say when love came and went,
I only know that summer sang in me
a little while, that in me sings no more.

TRANSITION

Autumn's music
is not just the breeze,
winding around indifferent trees,
shaking thick and twisted branches,
grabbing fistfuls of dying leaves
and letting them fall, spiralling
to the brown sodden earth below.

But footsteps squelching over
and through, the carpet of decay.
Is it just a prosaic sound
to those ears, who hear?
Or a warning to the unprepared?
The cold steel of winter
will soon be here!

PÅLANDSVINDEN

"Velveteen," said the grass to the wind
brushing her fingers through soft blades of green.
Bending each one, this way, then that,
rolling like waves on an emerald sea.
But Wind was silent; she did not reply
to the sassy grass, who wondered why?
The voice they knew, they heard it before
when Wind could create, a furious storm.

Wind continued her silent course
to the trees who stood at the end of the field.
A wondrous sound; a rhythm, and hum
as she caressed her way, through the canopy,
twisting thin branches and rustling leaves -
Wind felt the roughness of stately trees,
bark that remembered the seasons that came:
frigid cold snow, sunshine, and rain.

"Come, serenade us," said the trees to the wind,
"It's been far too long, not to hear you sing."
But Wind remained silent, traversing the trees,
for she had a date with the coast and the sea.

Beyond the deep forest lay a sandy shore,
and there did Wind, bellow and roar.
But not in anger, rage or despair,
she's just calling out to the sea, "I'm here!"

Upon the golden shore I sit - or stand
in all the seasons both night and day.
Listening to Wind's, soaring lullabies
with the tumbling waves on the bay.

GAEA'S LULLABY

Come to me and lay in my arms.

Come rest your heavy head and heart;

your weary flesh, and aching bones,

your pilgrim soul has traveled far.

On this gentle, rolling meadow;

refresh in spring's cool morning dew,

bathe in summer's tender caress,

clothe in the fall of autumn's hue.

Nor winter's icy breath or touch,

freeze or temper this boundless love.

We'll lie in a timeless embrace,

and awe the starry night above.

Snow
falls steadily.
Gaea's winter coat
protecting sleeping buds until
spring.

Snow,
dances across
the frozen lake,
with attitude and pirouettes.
Enchanting!

TWO ELFCHENS SNOW

MOONLIGHT

Twilight smoulders like an ember
as the blood moon slowly climbs.
Tranquil flames, bleeding crimson
between the earth and sky.
Like a fiery phoenix soaring
incandescent and iridescent
light, flickering silver through ash
whilst imperceptibly blending.

Crooked branches casting shadows
creep and grasp the fallow earth.
Mercurial wisps - tenuously
disperse into the chill night air.
Out upon the glistening bay
the restless main, slowly stirs
frigid waves that phantom kiss
a lover's broken heart away.

Moonwake softly emanates, on
bones that shore a barren soul.
Clutching sky, I embrace the night
and feel that I am not alone.
As heart and hands begin to tremble
I surrender, where land meets sea.
Submissive to her sweet caress
dispassionate, cold but gentle.

A WINTER'S JOURNEY

Bitter is the air, upon my face
its touch, chills both bone and marrow.
Death must feel, like this sensation
deep in the midst of frigid winter.
Far from home.

The ashen sky precipitates,
giant flakes tumbling and drifting down.
Snow on snow, on snow, on snow,
a dazzling blanket upon the ground.
Long to go.

Shoulder to shoulder, steadfast and true,
looms the forest of firs and cedars.
Gathering snow on evergreen boughs
sheltering, the weary traveller.
On the trail.

The eerie silence is deafening,
nature has fled or soundly sleeps.
Oblivious to the enchantment
or the careful crunch of heavy feet.
Through the snow.

As daylight slowly fades to grey,
the veil of snow is drawn to reveal,
a chill wind dancing with downy flakes,
glistening under evening's moonlight.
Glassy lake.

WINTER

Twilight casts then, its final palette,
flames of rouge upon the horizon.
Invoking memories of homely fires
in the comfort of, a lover's arms.
Winter's charms.

Beyond the lake, a flickering light;
pulse, now quickening and heartfelt yearn.
A welcoming sign; Hermione,
who sits and awaits for my return.
Hearts ablaze.

Warmth engulfs my frozen body
as winter melts from my tired bones,
raking the fire, a thousand sparks
framing your face, and our cosy home.
In your arms.

ABOUT THE AUTHOR

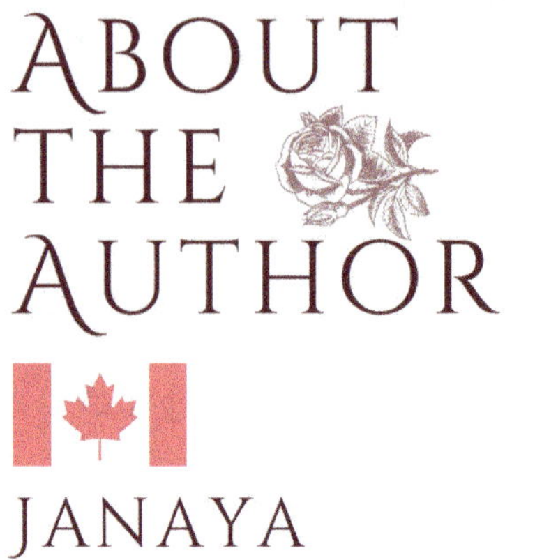

JANAYA STEPHENS (LG)

Janaya Stephens joined Instagram under the handle @throughthelookingglasspoet, which was quickly and endearingly shortened to "LG"—which has become her pen name.

She has always loved poetry and began writing at a very young age.
In university, she played for the varsity basketball team; sports have always been her passion.
Her majors were English literature and drama.
While at university, she was cast in the stage production of Romeo and Juliet and found her true calling. She then went to theatre school in Toronto and has since begun a successful career in film and television.
Janaya is a Canadian mother. She has a daughter and a son. When COVID hit, she was inspired to start writing again and discovered the poetry community on Instagram. It was there that she found enjoyment in reading others' poetry. Her live shows are popular, and her love of entertaining shines through.

Janaya's most poignant pieces seem to stem from her experiences as a mother and her love for them. Nostalgia and time are recurring themes, as is a good dose of self-reflection.

Janaya has just released her first book of poetry, A Little Red Book of Poetry, which is available on Amazon: https://mybook.to/Littleredbook

She is also working on a book of prose and short stories based on the true story of her experiences with her daughter when she was very ill and the ongoing challenges that they still face. Janaya has written a screenplay on the subject matter and a one-woman show for the stage. It just seems natural now to write a book.

- THE WINTER OF THE SOUL
- AUTUMN
- WINTER
- DEPTH OF THE VOID
- THE LONG, DARK WINTER
- DRIFTING
- HEAVY GREY
- THE LOOMING

JANAYA STEPHENS

JANAYA STEPHENS

THE WINTER OF THE SOUL

Under blankets of white—
that came in the night—
of already long dark days,
we huddled in without a way
from the blowing storm.

Another layer deep...
down...
down...
further down...
no strength for reaching
our slipping crowns.

Arms fatigued
drowning...
drowned...
the weight speaks volumes
in silent screams;
muffled by the depth of accumulation.
Absorbed within its housing;
the winter of the soul—
a bell's muted toll...

Liquid despair
filling lungs.
Nitrogen...
cooling...
pooling...
Sluggish via veins
a weak pulse remains;
in dire need of air,

in need of something...
from
somewhere.

AUTUMN

The Autumn wind that races through time and
trees brings with it a refreshing breeze.

Inevitably, to the season upon us;
a flash of brilliant colours to highlight
that spring is now long forgotten, and
a reminder that summer, and her
care-free ways, are no longer with us.

Instead, we are gifted with a seasoned beauty.
The colours are sharp and so bold!
One last dance before we fade—our memories,
dear, we hold.

*The autumn wind is the hand that guides the
aging leaves to the winter of their grassy graves.*

WINTER

Winter's chill—you are cold,
and you take hold in our now-fragile bones.
We long for a fire to sit by which to reminisce
about the warmth of youth—its glories and tribulations.
Our fireside friends; **Regret** and **Missing**,
hopefully, are joined by a **life well-lived**,
and a **heart full of love**.

JANAYA STEPHENS

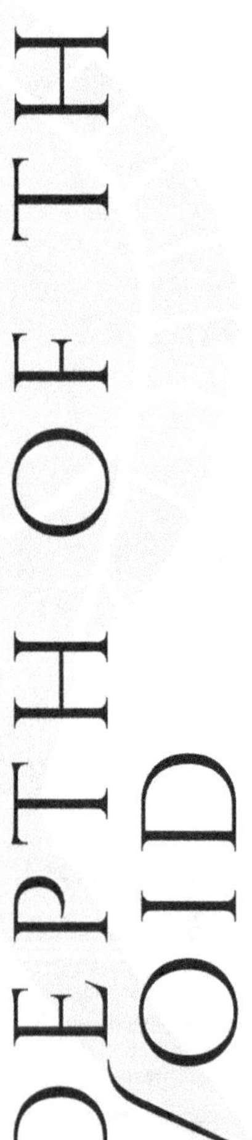

I'm soaking in the dripping questions
that linger, forming languid pools
that threaten to drown me.
A deep well—forming of questions.
No answers.

At night, with low light,
the glassy top of this collection of thoughts
is nothing but a reflection of *me*—
looking back at *me*—asking what it is I want.
And my answer hasn't changed,
even though I know
the game has been rearranged.

So the questions have gathered,
are gathering in great volume…
liters at a time,
an amount, immeasurable.

The increasing, unrelenting
emotions continually pending;
any given trigger
could have me sinking deeper,
and it is cold and unforgiving.

WINTER

Sometimes when the sun rises
—looking into this deep void
of questions with no answers—
I am blinded and need to turn my gaze.

Unable to see anything at all;
the dark reminding me,
then the light blinding...
what answers to the questions
will I be finding—
in the depth of this void?

For now, they just fester
in the languid pools,
by the clogged drain
of hope that remains.

COVID DIARIES
THE LONG, DARK WINTER

I feel like we're headed for—
a long, dark, winter...
of a year that will leave splinters;
in our minds and memories,
in our hands and feet,
in our hearts - for lack of chance
to unlock our lives and be free.

The broken night bleeding into our days.

The things we've seen—and the new way
I miss the smell of coffee
while writing in an artisan café.

I miss family gatherings;
celebrations and dinners.

I miss the moisture in my skin
as I've been bathing in disinfectant.

I miss a stranger's smile
when I pass them on the street.
I miss the children playing at the park
without needing to remind—

"six feet apart."

WINTER

A long, cold winter is heading this way.
We've been in its sister seasons;
trying to adjust to change
and make the most of **us.**

But now, the air is chilling;
shorter sun-filled days...
I'm losing my limber feeling.
A slow, creaking soul awakes each day—
struggling to make its way
to joy and purpose—that
leaves me longing
for the way, it was before.

Every day, that yearning;
like a weighted chain around my neck.
I can't break free, and it's burning—
a scar into my very being.

I cry inside, once a day,
in some big or small way.
Sometimes, tears streaming,
I open the window to let in light,
but change my mind... again.

I'm used to living in my cave, I fear,
with never any plans to steer.

A long, cold winter is nearing
and I'm already freezing.

JANAYA STEPHENS

I am **d**^{ri}**fting** through the days,
and it has been a minds-maze
of empty vacant tears,
and wishing—I had you near.

Winter is here, and it's been a year
since you held me, my dear.
Why do I still feel your touch
after we have been through

so

      very

           much?

The winds of change have blown in,
and it is now but a dream.
I still wonder if it's as you said,
"as you would have it seem."

A long-lost love song
now drifts on the breeze,
and washes over me.

I am lost in the woods of

   should

       could

          would...

DRIFTING

WINTER

You are *still* my *everything!*
But everything goes **nowhere**...
and this thought I must bear,
it's a weight on my back.

A *future, twisted in some lock,*
and I can not let it block—
as other opportunities, knock...

But for now, there is no door
through which I can walk,
because my heart is not free—
and I wonder if you feel like me?

How do I retrieve the key to my heart—
when from you it will not part?

Will I need to discover
you've chosen another?
Maybe that's a start...

I'm not sure I'm able
to otherwise believe
a future *without you*
...is even possible.

Think I need a new dream...
but, they are hard to find these days.
Maybe something will come
of springtime days—
I do fear though...

It will never feel **okay.**

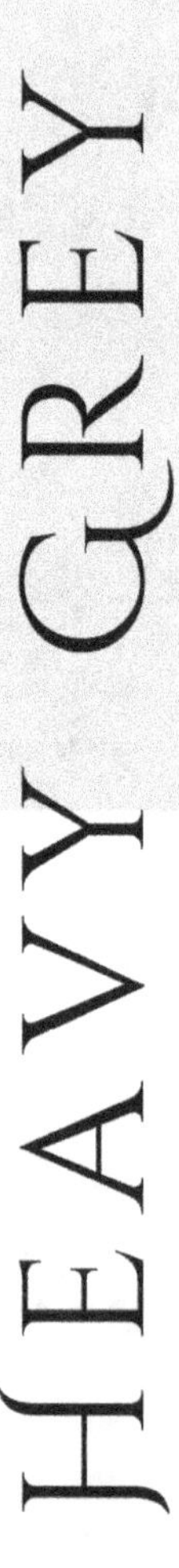

Heavy is my heart today,
a cloud of grey
that won't go away.
Meandering through,
I'm going to be "okay."

These things,
they come in waves.
I'm sure
I'll find my way.

Just ghosts of the past;
whispering to me quietly,
asking me questions,
passing their judgments,
reflecting my fears—
standing too close
to the bathroom mirror.

How did I get here?
Is here okay?

Somedays, I'm sure—
others, I'm not.
Feeling like, maybe
there are things I forgot.

Pieces of me here, and there,
scattered across the years...

The pieces sold.
The peace I bought.
The items, still on hold,
collecting dust on the shelf.

Somedays I just need to sit
quietly, with myself.

These things,
they come in waves.
Today is just a heavy, grey, day.

THE LOOMING

In the shrunken hours of sun,
after the festive fun,
there looms a feeling;
woven betwixt the bitter chills,
boxed in by wall and ceiling—
dropping its shadow cloak,
dressing you in feelings.

The adrenaline is gone.
You long for more.

It's the comedown.

I despise January.

Winter is here.
Without glitter and garlands.
Without lights and Yuletide.
The damp sadness of it.
Like the whole of the heart and brain
were not flesh at all,
but arthritic bone,
warning of the oncoming grey days.
A storm is brewing,
it's got you in its path,
and it's about to hit shore.

Worse these past years,
with daily virus scores—
nothing is like before.

My heart remembers, it's sore.

Now that my Fraser Fir
has started to shed
needles to the floor,
it's dying with the season,
and I will soon place it on the curb.
Then return the solo chair—with one red
pillow—to the corner in which
my beautiful tree shone brightly
bringing joy to me.

'Tis the oncoming storm.

Category, **unpredictable**.
Will it be a six, seven, or eight?
Will it crash through the gates—
the barricades I've placed?
Will they hold?
Did I secure them too late?

To what will it lay waste?
As I hunker down
...and **brace**.

About the Author

TODD WORRELL

Todd Worrell hails from North Carolina by way of Georgia. He started writing in 2019, at the age of forty-five and, draws inspiration from experience, memory, science, and mythology. His writing influences include Dante, DH Lawrence, TS Eliot, and several musical genres and lyric styles. In his free time, he enjoys reading about history and science topics, and tries to improve his guitar playing "skills."

He has two amazing daughters who bring him untold joy, and he currently shares his home with two dogs that adore him, and two cats that tolerate his existence.

Keep an eye out! My first book, *A Good Dark*, will be available on Amazon soon, titled

TODD WORRELL

TODD WORRELL

A PETITION IN DARKNESS

Can you help me maneuver away
from behind this blackout curtain
that envelopes me?

I've been pushing and pulling
for decades, this way and that—
to see clearly for once.

Chasing rays of light that escape,
yet unable to loosen its adhesive cling—
clawing and grappling to cast it aside.

He said resolutely; "I don't understand
string theory very much at all,
but we seem to share a frequency
that's hard to tune out
amidst the incessant bawls."

Always at a loss for words,
when there is so much to say.
Which words to convey,
without ends becoming frayed?

Pleated emotions,
bursting at their seams;
scrambling to untuck
underneath decorum's sheen.

She whispered to him, "I long to feel you
for the first time again—
to step foot across the emotional valleys
that we've managed to span."

A comfort in eyes,
and solace in a smile.

119

Needing the kneading of hands
and the easing of arms tightly
wrapped around.

"Let's kiss 'til we're both
weak in the knees
while we skylark under
the stars and sheets."

Unfurl this opaque and weighted cloth
and let me breathe tonight;
the ash to my oak,
under Milky Way light.

Come sing your lullaby, sweet ocean,
lap against my shore—
crash your waves within this heart
and marinate every pore.

.

WAVE OF DEPRESSION

Here I lie

shades drawn in broad daylight

on the made bed;

facing the wall,

shaking with tears,

convulsions in my chest—

hating my life.

Wanting something to stop

the misery;

a pill to make a zombie of me,

a permanent trip

into nothing-land.

No *feelings*.

No *disappointing*.

No *helplessness*.

No *impatience*.

Where everyone is a stranger,

and no danger lurks in my reality.

PERMAFROST

I was borne within
the permafrost;
in the frozen ground,
my soul has paused...

As slowly as the
glacier creeps,
this heartbeat— under
intransigent sheets of
ice in layers that steal
all warmth—
reducing my atoms to
death's lowest form.

I was never meant to
experience the thaw,
for this ice hides well
the tiniest of flaws.

It is here I have laid in
the sunniest shade,
and will reign until
nothing of life
remains.

COLD NIGHT

He enjoys the thrill of colder weather;
wearing shorts and t-shirts feels better—
while everyone else bundles and doubles
against the oft-icy wind's shuttle.

Twelve-o-six a.m. found him
thumbing through 35 mm pictures,
living in a shoebox from the 80s.

Satisfied upon paper, are images of her hand
holding letters to him;
the words of which he can never make clear,
a mixtape in the background,
still lying on her bed's surface.

But tonight (and more),
love is just another song in a silent playlist.

In those early morning hours—
when sleep is his abuser—
he will make his way to the kitchen and
shuffle with intent through the junk drawer;
the pens, batteries, stray pieces of paper,
like adolescent memories
that he was resolute,
(at the time)
that he would return to...

but only when it was propitious to do so.

If only the nuts would match these bolts!
Small screwdrivers that belonged with the others,
(only a few steps away),
a nearly-empty roll of tape,
(with little more than an allusion to adhesion),
a picture hanging kit,
(still unopened),
and anchors of varying styles,
(for attaching unattainable goals to his walls).

But there is another cold,
indubitably bound,
closer to life than his imagination alleges,
(for which he dons many more layers than he
possesses),
to keep himself whole,
pound for pound.

MIND, DARKNESS, AND LIGHT

My mind is set in a story from Poe,
gothic, foggy, and unbearably cold;
I haven't seen as much as some,
just enough to know—
when the clouds are coming.

I've seen through the dark,
an emptiness in hearts,
stared evil in the eye—
and I grin while it hides,
then haunts,
and longs to win.

The questions are empty, and
all of the answers, puerile,
the meaning once sought,
now charred in some fire.

>>**Doubt has always been the beast
shoveling dirt on my back,
designed to perform
with the tools of my craft,
like when I called you that time
but hung up the line
and left my heart dying
on the south-facing side** <<

I used to stare at the stars at night,
now I watch the ground;
where the dance of life
carries on,
without...

No longer making believe
in the shapes of clouds,
but watching the silhouette of the rain
as it falls about.

"To the victor go the spoils.

but even the prey must sustain."

My head is below the surface;
I've been punished before—
drowning with company,
arms-length from the shore.

Today it was the little things,
tomorrow the void twists;
I'll shuffle down the sidewalk
waving at my former wishes.

My mind is colder than before,
shivering at certain thoughts—
hiding from others all the more.
It scoffs at independence,
blaming duality for its pain,
if only it could hemorrhage sadness,
and let it pour from every vein.

    >> It's dark over here
      turn on the lights
      I've been holding my arms out
      in search of...
      let me show you...
      hush for a second...
      I feel the wind humming
      and the moon laughs...

      do you hear it?
      tonight? <<

FRIGID ECSTASY

Winter waves its ferocious wand,
stirring viscous vibrations
between the eagerness and fear of
our forlorn emotional momentum.

My diminutive heart,
still swallowed by snow—
preserved in a jar of icy formaldehyde;
January's bitter-most juice.

What I need is:

* *your scented symphony—*
an orchestral heat,
a writhing aria—to be salted
in the evaporative harmonies
of seduction unleashed!

* *A well-seasoned melting*
of our mutual cages—having long
been carved from cold;
as we feast on the fresh, succulent
fruits of a longing—
both flirtatious, and bold.

* *Our tongues, like flickering tails,*
anticipating anxious release;
as we empty the ether of galaxies
under passion's inviting canopy—
and a faint light leaks
from the leaves of our post-Edenic state.

Both thrown into tomorrow,
naked but unashamed;
my meaning, my entirety,
now nailed to your name.

ON CHANGING SEASONS

**"This was the way things were
always meant to be"**, she thought.

The sun (somewhat) overhead;
winter's southern exposure—warmed her
in ways, the high sun of summer could not.

Flashbacks and snippets of time
flutter like wind-ruffled pages in her book.
She grinned and remembered; those paragraphs
never **quite** flesh out the full plot
now, do they?

With a handbag of regrets and missed chances—
things that made sense before,
now choked like the mariner's necklace.

The weight of her hours, swimming in
the stagnation of this-or-that day, as she is
taking stock of her space;
what to do and what to say.

**There's a place, (or so she understood),
between breaths...**

**where emotion still flutters before air
fills the vacuum once more;**

**and in the heart's diastolic pause—
a few of her favorite memories stutter—**

**then the blood rushes forth
and begins with another.**

ABOUT THE AUTHOR

S.A. QUINOX

S.A. Quinox is a young Belgian poet, philosopher, and student of the paranormal. She writes for the broken among us. Quinox is a beginning yet growing poetess that is known for her beautifully deep yet melancholic words which have the ability to wreck your heart and then glue it back together again.

At a young age, she had already discovered her love for writing. What first started off as suicide notes, later on, transformed into the poetry she writes today. Quinox has a unique way of designing her own books. She always chooses black pages to preview her style.

By doing so, she makes her readers delve deeper into the abyss of her words.

Besides poetry, she also aspires to be a spiritual person. Quinox enjoys learning about the paranormal arts and takes classes from professional masters. She enjoys learning about things like Crystal Healing, Reiki, Demonology, spiritual protection, spiritual cleansing, and various forms of divination. In daily life, she finds a lot of pleasure in connecting with nature and animals.

Quinox loves to respond to messages so please do not shy away from conversation!

Find her at Facebook.com/SAQuinoxPoetry

or on Instagram.com/QuinoxPoetry

S.A. QUINOX

THE LONELY TABLE

I wished we didn't
gaze into the depths
of these plates;
instead I wished we
reached over this
lonely table—
reached for the soul
behind these sacred bones,
held hands above candlelight,
instead of dripping sorrow
above flames that no longer
warm the cold sting—
of a family no longer whole.

BOTTLES ON CHRISTMAS EVE

My heart tumbles
into the shards
of empty bottles,
I escape into their cavern,
and I find my reflection
stuck at their bottom.

Far deeper than flesh—
deeper than the love that
once tied your eyes to mine,
and my hands to yours.

Holidays are a time
of celebration,
but even with your
warm body next to mine-
I feel alone.

About the Author

Angela Psalm

Wominjeka All!

(Hello in the Woiwurrung language of the Wurundjeri People from the Kulin Nation, traditional owners of Melbourne from my hometown in Australia).

My name is Angela, some know me as the *Dungeon Mistress* or *The Psalm.*

My Instagram account @angela_psalm

My love of writing began at the tender age of 10 while journaling my emotions and reading the many sci-fi - fantasy adventure books which I consumed as I loved being lost in far away lands. I found my love in Arthurian Legend and Sonnets with Shakespeare but truly found kindred souls with Jane Austen and the Bronte Sisters. Yet published, I am currently writing my first novel.

ANGELA PSALM

Here stands a sentient, evergreen, coniferous tree,
the annual soul, cultivating an essence of pine.
Each contorted branch, a symbol of family,
the scent of monoterpene-limonene entwined.

Each veneer filled with lights of sensory memory,
sparking an everlasting allusion to happiness,
a melding freshness of cool, mintiness reverie.
An illumination of star, ornamental headdress,

representing the birth of our savior, Nazarene;
gifted gold, frankincense, and myrrh expressed—
in turn, we gift our loved ones in remembrance, glean,
willing a new year ahead for this evergreen to be blessed.

A Conifer of Ancestry

THE RESURRECTION OF A VERDANT GROVE

Barren fields have sparked

this seedling's growth,

nil—held in a whirl of a life

filled with hope.

To the stars, every breath ambit

filled in heavenly grace.

Two-Zero-Twenty-Two illuminates

and enumerates in ones, Cronos face;

Verdant vales etched in ebony

and gold leaf scribe, knots of truth;

cosmic purveyors—a nebula of dreams

and epiphanies coup,

A dendro sprite, who has watched

centuries of stars implode and give birth;

as the world around me grows, I feel it

rumble with acknowledgment, to be one

with my worth.

AUBURN EQUINOX

Autumn comes in the perpetual veil of recurring memoirs,
where the beginning of the missing vesper
is an uninterrupted gorgeous instigate of sunsets,

There we find a war of the hemispheres;
as one sprouts new growth in late seasons,
the other produces an array of burnt hues.

Oh, dear September, you are the sweetest curse;
reminding us of our seasonal blues.
Your breezes feel like squalls in our untimely demise,
while the petrichor of our soul treads in one's false hope—
a weightless love within the abandonment of desires—
which sits in incomplete diary entries, our sacred interlope.
There our hearts were made of stardust and fireflies—
an untamable fire that begins in the depth of my rib cage.

Do I still have a home in you?
Or will I be counting our last breaths
in the demise of the emotional undead?
A psithurism of dashed, broken hearts
with blunt edges as they mark my heart 'out of order.'
In midst of the dying, 'longing' is my middle name.
There sits my poetry on your lips,
your mark that signals you are mine.

But alas, someone has to leave first,
as we start to settle in a chamber of my worst secrets,
we viewed our love spill all over...
another victim,
another Grecian tragedy,
and in my limerence weakness—
I knew it would always be you.

PALIMPSEST SOVEREIGN

Lilium of sleeping winter's day,
set adrift in an acrimonious affray—
frozen deep in a glacier of haunting sorrow,
her lithium of sadness is preserved in the absence of tomorrow.

A princess in unheralded forlorn,
harrowing blizzard of the cataclysmic storm;
she walks the path of a caged cold moon, once loved—
frigid laser-luster dancing in a pool of her own blood.

Virginal white skin, black, coal heart therein,
ornamented diamond teardrops of crystalline grace,
dovelike coos emitted from primal cries in a longing embrace.

Papered avarice laced,
scar-draped shoulders, chaste,
heartless, interlaced whispers of despondent insanity,
For **you**—were the precipitation of my melancholy and atrophy
of concupiscence in blasphemy.

LADY OF WINTER

My enchanted flower, frozen in ice,
screams for an opportunity in life—
but you will neither age nor decay.

In a glacier, your essence is locked away,
while you infuse each fiber of my being.

You are cold and numb to all feeling.

You are my beauteous lady of winter,
the dark little secret of a turpitude sinner.

CROWDED RESURRECTION

I am born of murdered lies—
watched them grow wings and caw their cries.
Felt my void reach for the dawning of light,
awakening my third eye to a diaphanous night.

Food, for worms, I give unto the earth,
vegetative facets lead to our rebirth.
Sing to me into the limerence of dulcet happiness,
amassing beauty in the twilight of my darkness.

See me fly towards the heavens sunrise,
a psithurism encouraging us towards cerulean skies.
I hear the harp of hope from trauma, performing an opus for me,
welcoming me home towards the palace of eternity.

Scarlet, my enlightened soul,
has rent my bones,
and she's stranded in a
winter coat of sorrow;
with despondency and
desolation thorns to care,
its dark horse twists tightly
the backseat thoughts of the morrow.

There's a lot about me
you have to accept as unknown;
one of them is how my scent
is that of the sweetest rose.
I watch you, my love, and am
drinking affirmations as a slow burn.
The blood-soaked cupid bows are wedged
within the earth, I yearn.

As I gather my strength
to bolster our union's breath,
silently a night under the moon—
the stars call your name and it resonates.
I am entranced by your glorious being—
wrapped around my twisted stems.
Mellifluously, the chorus of our love
transmitting to Heaven's gems.

WINTER'S ROSE

SNOWSTORM

*Your words preceded the
blizzard of my heart.
Cold, frozen in an emotional
snowstorm set apart.*

ECCLESIASTICAL UTTERANCE

You once said that the world is a better place
because of me, that when you held me in your arms,
you tasted freedom—and in those moments,
the only wants were each other, that we lived life
like an ecclesiastical utterance, that we had
traversed in wasted lands, but found the beauty in
everything.

You were my amnesty, my Polaris.
I will not spend my life in regrets or fathomless
sorrow—for I was blessed, blessed to have known
what love could be.

I didn't need to dream this was once my reality,
I knew to survive, I could not sit in the space of
remiss, but I still wished I could hold you just once
more—away from the solitary abandonment.

But instead, I was incessantly bereft; I had been the
one left in identifying you, dashed from trauma, but
holding onto hope...

but I heard it go, **BANG!!!**

Down the barrel, your life was measured through
the telescopic sight.

A pure soul now encased in lead.

In his image, the reaper wept; while I tried to find solace
in forgiving—I closed my eyes away from darkness,
I dreamt that your life was still as bright and present.
Then I opened my eyes and with a smile on my face,
moved my searching hand across to your side of the bed.
Then came the waves of aching pain—and unearthly sobs
escaped these lips.

The ones you once kissed...
yet another cruel reminder that you were gone,
and inside me all that I am felt dead.

So, I thought of happier times with you;
you had become my Lazaris stone, brought meaning to
this and safety in the afterlife.

I will not let the memory of you be tainted;
even when it flies in the face of justice,
even when my humanity has been parted like the red sea—
I will switch life off of its destruction,
I will switch life on determined revelation,
I will tend to the garden of sensibility
I will never forget the feel of your skin,
an aphrodisiac of treasured memory—
as I bathe in the holiest of lights and focus on all things
that will make me happy.

Even with only half of me.

About the Author

Barbara Soehner

Barbara Soehner is a New York Native, having grown up and enjoyed a full life in the bustling city with all its glorious culture and energy. This might very well be why she has enjoyed a lively career in the arts. She attended college at Marjorie Webster majoring in speech, drama, radio, and T.V. After graduating Barbara quickly landed commercial and voice-over jobs. She learned the guitar, started writing songs and singing and added that to her artistic portfolio. You can hear many of Barbara's songs on Soundcloud under Barbara Soehner.

Barbara went back to school and graduated with a BA from Marymount Manhattan College and an LCSW from Fordham University becoming a social worker. Once again she returned to school attaining a certificate in psychoanalytic psychotherapy and opened her private practice.

Barbara has enjoyed sharing her own life experiences through poetry. She has found a beautiful community on Instagram where she hosts lives that have become very popular. Her reading voice draws many in the poetry community to hear their work read by her and enjoy her many fascinating life stories as well.

You can find Barbara on Instagram @barbara_soehner

Her book 'The Glittering Bird Reborn' is available on Amazon in paperback and kindle format and audiobook format on Apple Books and Audible.

BARBARA SOEHNER

A journey so long—
filled with wintry storms;
harsh and brutal sleet,
cold and piercing rain,
wet and melting snow.
Not at all unlike your;
harsh and brutal lies,
cold and piercing eyes,
wet and melting love.
A journey so long.

A journey so long—
and yet I hang on
like a summer night's
long and languishing breeze,
sparkling and vivid stars,
beautiful glorious moon.
Not at all unlike my fantasy of your;
long and lingering kisses,
sparkling and vivid laugh,
beautiful, glorious, embrace.
A journey so long.

The journey goes on—
Lies and lies, such deceit!
Falseness and pretense
entering the windows
of my soul;
killing my goodness,
sucking at my smile
'til it fades and leaves
my face.

A journey so long—
Will it end for me now?
Will I free myself from
this bumpy place,
this darkened road to nowhere?
A journey so long.
We will see.

CONCRETE POEM
ICICLES

Icicles, such funny people!
 (I know they're not people,
  but they have such a
personality!) They
  hang there in the
   cold and develop
    into a shape. Only
     they know why they
      became that shape.
      I like icicles! They
      remind me
    of myself;
  they're just all
 alone and
   happy. Yes,
    sometimes,
      they annoy
       me when
       they

     drip

       drip

     drip

       drop

       on my
     head when I'm walking
    underneath. Who likes a big,
   cold drop falling on their head?
  I like icicles they remind me of... me!
 Happy and free to be whatever they
        choose to see.

BARBARA SOEHNER

CHRISTMAS EVE

How easily you forget me as if I never was.
It's Christmas Eve and this year,
my heart has died a little more.

You were such a precious gift—
a miracle when you came into my life.
Such a joy. So much happiness.

I wasn't going to realize this...
to express my sorrow so openly,
for all the world to see—

but it is Christmas Eve!
Emotions are huge and flowing, and I realize
you are not going to be in touch.

I wish I understood why,
perhaps that would help.
I hope you are happy and safe.

I asked Santa to bring a message from you;
I prayed to God for this Christmas gift.
I am proud I have the guts to say this—

if I keep it inside I will drown in tears.

SOMETHING HAS DIED INSIDE

I am like a dying flower in a beautiful vase;
all the other flowers are continuing to thrive
but you have to water me to keep me alive—
to give me permission, to be.

So shall I pretend I am someone else?
Shall I pretend I have a love I don't have?
Will that help me live again?

Searching for the answer through miles of road.
Confused, searching for the reason
why I became so sick, anyway.

I think the words old and alone
go together, like—
I never would have guessed I would wind up here.

I am a flower, once desperately loved.
I am a beautiful heart, sadly disposed of and forgotten.
I am like a dying flower in a beautiful vase.

BARBARA SOEHNER

MAGIC OF CHRISTMAS

I think the most magical thing about **Christmas**
is the fascination in a child's eyes.

Such a little girl I was, in a brand new house.
It was Ma Mere's house—she was my
stepmother's mother.

I will never forget the excitement of seeing the
Christmas tree, it was the first one I'd ever
seen.

They let me be part of decorating it; holding
those shiny glass balls, and carefully placing
them on the tree branch—was wonderful fun!

Yes indeed, for a child Christmas is magic!
For me as a tiny girl, it was a gift of joy.

Do you ever wonder
how you can stop sadness?
Do you ever wonder
why some days are so hard?
Do you ever have a feeling
you just want to die—
because things seem so bleak,
that you just want to cry?

Do you ever wonder why
you are even here?
Why you have to face so much fear?
Do you ever wonder...
I don't know,
although... I think
I do a lot of wonder

Do you ever look up at the sky
to search for miracles?
Do you find them?
I wonder if it's possible
to look inside a star?
When you hear it call your name
do you feel its magic pull,
trying to make you feel sane?
Such a crazy time for me—
so many unanswered questions.
Do I ever wonder?
Yes, I do.

DO YOU EVER WONDER

Let's ask ourselves, *"what is a hug?"*
We all know it's a wonderful feeling when
someone's arms sweep around you,
hold you tight.

But, really...

What **is** a hug?

Well, I guess you could say it's an embrace;
it's joy, it's love, it's happy,
it makes you feel giggles,
it makes you feel wanted and appreciated,
it makes you melt
inside your heart...
deep inside.
A hug is JOY!

A hug is a giant gift from your child.
There is nothing like it...
nothing.

You feel their arms squeeze you tight—
with all their might.
Things they can't utter easily, **are there** in their
beautiful hold.

My beautiful son...
his hug is the one
I miss the most.

A hug is a flower you receive.
You may be hurting,
the flower hugs you with its beauty.

You save it forever.

It dries and crumples.

Its love is always.

The world is crying now;
the one thing I see as I watch the streams of
sadness? Everyone hugs and tries so hard to
love, to soothe.

Hugs are free!
Thank God for hugs!

BARBARA SOEHNER

SEE THE STARS

See the stars, so high?
Many memories have crossed their eyes;
they've watched a smile turn and cry,
they saw me lose your love—
it wasn't the first time,
there were two before.
But I mustn't give up hope, there's a reason!
Though the years are slipping by... it isn't easy.

Looking at the stars, so high, I'll hold on to my soul.
I've worked on my career, but now I need a home.
I want so much to have a tiny friend I can call my own;
a little baby boy or girl, I've waited oh, so long.

I never heard you cry.
You were born too young to say goodbye.
The doctor said, "I'm sorry I can't save her."
Oh, your father standing there
watching you be born, it was very sad.
The midwife asked me "would you like to see her?"
I said, "yes" and they let me hold you.

Looking at the stars so high, I'll hold on to my soul.
I've worked on my career, but now I need a home.
I want so much to have a tiny friend I can call my own;
a little baby boy or girl, I've waited oh, so long.
A little baby boy or girl, that I can call my own.

See the stars so high? I see the stars so high,
many memories have crossed their eyes.

Oh the moon, the moon!
Such a strong force in our lives,
sometimes I wonder,
"Who is there for you?"
"Are you alone, Mr. Moon?"
"Do you need a hug?"

No, I don't think so;
you've guided so many people
for so many years.
For eternity you've been there.
Sweet moon,
I just want you to know that I love you.
I love looking up at you.
I love feeling your light on my face.
when you're full.
I love the fact that I can count on you,
for you will never go away!
You are always there.
You will always stay.

If you are ever sad,
I will pick you out of the sky,
I will hold you when you cry.
Yes, sweet moon,
I give you a big hug.

I thank you so much, for your love.

I WILL HOLD YOU WHEN YOU CRY

BARBARA SOEHNER

I am on my way to the battlefield
inside the cage that holds my heart.
My heart has been wounded many times,
I must rescue it.
I have found a wishbone; a powerful weapon.
Broken correctly... all your wishes come true.
I can't go wrong with that!

So I will arm myself with this wishbone—
I will dive into the cavity of my heart;
I shall soothe it and tell it, "don't worry
happiness is coming, it really is."

Something tells me times are changing for me.
It's been rough, so rough
but there's a little glimmer of hope, I see.

I have told myself again and again to;
**"stop worrying, stop wondering, start hoping,
JUST BE."**

I went to a costume store.
I looked through all the racks.
I found a beautiful flowing gown and a crown;
I will dress myself as a queen!

I will jump on top of a beautiful white stallion
and march into the rib cage of my heart.
I will be armed with my magic wishbone, filled
with all of my dreams.
I will place it inside the rib cage, where my heart
lives.

I *will* succeed.

As I feel the first chilly breeze,
I want to run inside where I'll be safe.

The cold brings back memories;
memories of a frozen heart
that never thawed.

Icicles thaw and slowly drop
to the ground.
Where do they go?

Broken hearts shrivel and hide.

Life is hard sometimes;
memories of loss you can't
forget—they come back when it's cold.

Darkness falls early.

I hide inside.

SEASONAL BLUES

About the Author

Julie Ann Keleher

I am a poet who loves Midnight and Coffee, and all the strange things in life. I am also a mother of two amazing children. I love spending time with family and friends. I started writing when I was seven years old about magical worlds where nobody would suffer. I am an advocate for many different health issues and for the elderly. I tell all my secrets to the moon, and the stars hold onto my prayers. "Poetry is not just a word, poetry is meant to be heard! " When I see something I just love I say, "Oh now that's "mykindamidnight" !

Instagram handle @mykindamidnight

JULIE ANN KELEHER

MAGNIFICENT WEAVER

Let us weave our tapestries of love and life
into signs and patterns of the beauty of this
universal world; where the dew drops grace the
magnificent web in which we are all connected,
past, present, and future.

Time—consuming of what was, what is, and what
will be—hanging onto moments we had in our life;
entwining soft, magical pieces; letting go of the
bitterness and strife.

Let the part of the web that has lost its glimmer
blow away, then spin together another piece—so
gracefully it shimmers.

How delicately we flow through our time of tough
sorrows, so always a new web can be spun for a
beautiful tomorrow.

SHADOWS

The shadows from
the leftover leaves show a way,
for the scurry of the squirrel
still finding a nut astray.

The shadows of
the clouds hiding the sun,
let us know time has changed
for everyone.

The shadows bouncing
off the walls,
from the children, now dancing
in their bedrooms and halls—
let us know the end
of the season is near,
so embrace each other
for another well-lived year;
before it becomes just a **shadow**,
and you say, "I was once here..."

MY CHRISTMAS TREE

I want to be your Christmas tree!
Please, be gentle when you put
your hooks in me;
make sure to use **both hands** when
you add the lights.

I am smaller at the top,
so when you get to the bottom,
be sure to cover me just right.

Gently add the garland for my limbs
to perfectly show, I want to sparkle
with the lights; so when people see
me—the truth they will know; I am
your tree covered with love.
...

And from there, go to all the bulbs;
add them in such a fashion they will
twinkle like the stars!

You must not forget the candy canes
to make me sweet and delicious;
I want to always please you,
make sure you lick your lips for those
candy cane kisses!

Then add the bows to make me look
just like a gift to you every day.
Oh! How I want to be so perfect for
you in every shape and every way!

Last, but truly not the least, the angel
goes on top; to truly remember all we
have, instead of what we haven't got.

ABOUT THE AUTHOR

CLEOPATRA FERNHILL

Cleo, the quintessential romantic with stars in her eyes, has always loved poetry and words. She's been writing poetry seriously for the last few years.

She's a mom, teacher, poet, and gardener.

Her poems depict the beauty of being loved, loving, the tragedy of love lost, longings, the beauty, and mystery of the moon and stars, the cosmos, nature, flowers, wild gardens, deep feelings, and deep connections. She loves fairytales and myths and full moon nights and dancing in the moonlight.

As an elementary school teacher, she loves teaching the little ones and especially loves teaching them art.
After writing poems, she loves gardening, decorating, and playing with paper and paint.

Cleo loves living in the Pacific Northwest. She has a grown son who is the joy of her life and her greatest encourager and her number-one fan! He started all of this in 2020, when he said, "Mom, you need to join Instagram and share your poetry there."

Every day, she smiles and says, "I have found my soulmates here on insta and I'm so grateful. Thank you beyond words, my precious son." Thank you too, beautiful insta poets and artists, for your love and support and for being here with me through the joy and the loss in my life.

CLEOPATRA FERNHILL

WITHOUT YOU

CLEOPATRA FERNHILL

Our pockets overflowed with pennies and prayers
offering all we had to buy just one more night
of magic together.

Time was a broken mirror of shattered dreams,
deaf to our bargaining,
a sinister, shadow overlord,
uncaged and on the prowl that night,
relentless,
knew our address.

This silence that is in the starry sky, cradles me
and the sleep that is among these lonely hills
still taunts me,
stirring up these pangs of loneliness.
I'm helpless, cocooned in thoughts of you,
wrapped in somber shades of November.
I surrender to the darkness of this starless night,
held by winter's woeful wings,
sundered from the light.

How effortlessly the shadows overtake my thoughts,
steal the sunshine,
casting dark spells on my days and my nights.
Silver moon holds my grieving heart,
can't heal me now,
perhaps he'll subdue the hands of time,
stop all the clocks,
wake us from this nightmare.

The vacant sky looms above me, swirling,
holds secrets of autumn leaves'
last dance before dying.
You are gone forever.
It feels like the last summer day on Earth.

I loved you completely and you loved me the same.

That's all, the rest is confetti.

My winter breaths erase and unwind yesterday's tunes,
then recreate them over, again and again,
begging the fortune teller for one more chance
to change our fate.

I'm lost without you.

You're the poetry that lingers on my tongue,
among the shattered pieces of my heart.
Silk words, sighs, and tears drift among
clouds of memories saturated with you.

I feel your unseen eyes,
hear your gentle voice in my desolate dreams,
as the weight of this emptiness speaks to my broken heart—
an immeasurable loss I could never have imagined.

When the breeze kissed you its final kiss
and a thousand stars dimmed,
midnight beckoned you as we held you close,
counted your last shallow breaths.

That early, sunless morning,
ineffable feelings of heartbreak
took root in our broken hearts.
Like a sleepy, autumn mist you faded,
succumbed to death
so gently,
without a sound.

Your deep, blue eyes still haunt me.

My desperate heart longs for you.

BREATHING WINTER

I drink you in like sunshine on my skin,
ever so slowly, savoring the warmth of you.
I'm no longer a misplaced, frozen rose;
blooming alone in the icicle breaths of lost loves,
cradled in snowstorm's lullabies,
retracing my dreams like invisible footsteps on the snow.

Until the cold becomes a precious gift of hopeful stars,
a crystal forest of delight;
not sad, faded, photographs of past winter landscapes
of frozen hearts—I'll remain wandering glitter trails
lit by a cold moon, wearing a hibernating halo,
lost in an icy bower overflowing
with evergreen longings for you.

I drink you in like sunshine on my skin;
remember countless delights in your embrace,
the full moon's secrets we shared the music of your sighs.
I succumb to the promise of this new, winter dawn
knitted in starry silences of pirouetting
snowflakes of memories;
effervescent, gossamer dreams of belonging.
Habits of frost gently etch winter's rhapsody
on distant bells kissed by wintry breath.
Invisible strings of midnight magic
take root in my heart, ignite the glowing wildfire
of my love!

This beauty, this dance, this poetry your body creates,
touches like stardust kissed constellations, delirious,
spinning, twirling, dancing together.

You're all I see,
my eyes, my heart, fill only with you.

I drink you in like sunshine on my skin,
enraptured, lost in the poetry of your irresistible,
tantalizing touch.

LONGINGS

Melancholy thoughts, like dying butterflies
remembering their summer days,
the last sip of sweetest nectar,
flitter-flutter,
lost in a penumbra of deep, indigo haze.

The moon in Pisces sighs
feels our lament,
smiles among glistening stars this sultry, summer night;
breathes passion into our once-entombed hearts,
now unchained, set free.

You caught me like a mythical mermaid
in your net of immeasurable longings,
fiery hot.

Your heart, a universe.
Your eyes, like opals.

You, a lonely fisherman lost at sea,
praying for the gift of someone to
return his love,
touch his skin,
quench his thirst,
never leave.

Descendants of mercurial shadows,
who once danced with us in the moonlight—
weep and call out your name.

No one answers.

Only the sounds of my tremulous heart beating,
echoing through amber, windswept leaves—
are heard.

**I breathe in the sorrow,
the unbearable ache,
remembering the last time I heard your voice.**

Golden dawn refuses to shine.

Ancient remnants of past memories
pound on the door of my heart;
haunting my sleep,
invading my dreams,
in this alien land - without you here with me.

The universe has come undone.

Stars tumble.

I forget to breathe.

Nothing feels the same.

SHADOWS

The moon and I whisper your name.

We're lost in daydreams of you,
can't fathom this vast emptiness—
like a vacant sky, longing for its glistening stars.

Your memory infuses my heart.
Oh, how I long to feel your loving gaze—
brightening my days.

Oh, how I long to see your smile—
hear your laugh,
feel the warmth of your touch,
warming my nights.

I'm lost without you.
My heart is held in winter's frigid embrace.

Never have I felt so alone.
Never have my days and nights been so dark.

Each season I'm mourning the inconsolable loss of—

you.

Your memory is etched on my heart
and on my skin.

There'll never be another, you.

FOREVER

Sandcastles are evanescent.
Dreams are like fog's dim memory;
forgetting his favorite mountain to climb,
or where he left his keys,
or the name of your favorite flower.

I'm not a tourist here spying on villagers,
begging for directions,
my copper cup, empty.
I know the meaning of forever,
(it's my favorite perfume)
and the way a full moon captivates
and infuses your every breath.

I'll walk you home, **or carry you**,
place you by the fireside,
remembering your name.

I've never been afraid of strangers
who color their world in shades
of the shape of their hearts.

I'll respond to you in your
love language, and make your every
dream come true, tonight.

When the fire has dimmed to embers,
casting silhouettes of tired dancers on the wall,
I'll sing you to sleep—
as I whisper your name into my dreams,
hoping you know the meaning of ***forever***.

Howling moon, endlessly captivating.
Reciprocal emotions heal the midnight sky,
leave traces of stardust shimmering.

Our oaths, resplendent against red, plum,
and cashmere clouds.

A forest of breathing trees—
overflowing with murmurings
of sapphire butterflies', rendezvous—
listens for our heartbeats, buried under avalanches of time;
caresses me as the full, silver moon sings a lullaby
in branches swaying.

Time is magically stuck in a slow-motion snow globe,
breathing heavily.

That night, we became lovers, the moon and I,
enticed by the ink stains tantalizing,
alive on our fingertips.

Moonbeams aching to be heard, slowly unravel—
flow into the midnight depths of me.

Irresistible alphabets dance in our mouths
hungry for love—create a winter rose
with their sentient ink.

Under a dark spell no longer,
or haunted by residual aches from the past,
enchanted stars thread the sky like fairy lights,
acquiesce in the jubilant, wintry silence.

Obsidian night gasps,
chokes on the pervading loneliness.

Swirling clouds inhale the darkness;
cry over parched land of cold, lifeless, statues.

A tiny parcel,
with only sad, stone cherubs as friends,
one vase of wilted flowers overturned,
faded—

and a lone silhouette lost in silent prayer.

Gravedigger wipes his eyes,
asks permission to plant flowers there.

He kneels over her,
bears his soul, mourns and weeps,
begs to take her place.

Said he remembers her beautiful, dark eyes
and the glistening stars they contained.

ALONE

An anchor,
rhinestone studded,
a dime store attraction,
a flame to the moth
that lives inside of you and me.

Silently bequeathed
to each generation,
softly in shadows of lullabies,
birthday balloons,
and stuffed teddy bears.

Vast as the sky.

Sometimes parading
as a kind zephyr,
sometimes a hungry, mad,
evolving hurricane,
but never forgotten.

Love; learned right or wrong,
offered to thirsty hearts begging
for a mirror, a key, an open gate,
a flowered path, a drop of sunlight,
a ray of water, or
ANYTHING
to break the loneliness,
the misunderstanding, and chaos—
brewing like a stew
in a lonely kitchen
on a winter afternoon.

About the Author

Karen Slaughter Steiner

Karen Slaughter Steiner is now retired. Formerly, she had jobs as a piano teacher, a music specialist at a school, a secretary, and as a school assistant. Karen graduated from Fort Wayne Bible College in 1979 with a Bachelor of Music. Several years ago, Karen received a diagnosis of Parkinson's Disease which has radically changed her life. She has lost most of her skills playing the piano because of this cruel disease. Since her creativity still needs an outlet, she has turned to the wonderful world of words.

Since she was a young girl, Karen has loved to read and has devoured many books that have enriched her life. She loves the sounds the words make and the magic of putting just the right words together. In college, she learned to love Haiku, and her husband claims that she thinks in Haiku. Karen loves studying languages. In addition to her native English, she is currently learning Spanish and Ukrainian. Other interests include singing, reading, word puzzles, jigsaw puzzles, diamond painting, and cats.

Karen lives in Fort Wayne, Indiana. She has a husband who plays the trumpet, and a son who is a wonderful violinist. She also has two cats who add a lot of joy to her life. Clementine the Clever is a senior citizen cat who loves to lie in a sunny window, take naps, and cuddle with her humans. Amelia the Adventurous is aptly named after Amelia Earhart. She adores playing, running through tunnels, finding trouble, and trying to entice Clementine to play. Amelia also loves to snuggle.

The most important thing in Karen's life is her relationship with her Lord and Savior, Jesus Christ. She is thankful for the blessings God has given her. She is also grateful for the talents He has given her and that although one talent, playing the piano, seems to be gone, the need for creativity has been filled with writing poetry. Soli Deo Gloria.

KAREN
SLAUGHTER
STEINER

A LAMENT FOR THANKSGIVING

Traditionally, a pumpkin represents the holiday of Thanksgiving.

Perhaps, instead, it should be a **squash**.

Why a squash?
Because, increasingly, Thanksgiving is being **squashed** between Halloween and Christmas.

Thanksgiving sometimes seems like an oversight; sure, most people still have a turkey dinner on the day itself, but stores put away anything about Thanksgiving sometimes *a whole week* before the actual day. When I asked an employee about it, he replied that they were ordered to get rid of Thanksgiving, and get ready for a big Christmas— then he gave me a sheepish grin.

My city used to light a beautiful Christmas tree the day **after** Thanksgiving, but this year the lighting will take place **before.**
Also, Thanksgiving is overshadowed by the mega-shopping event known as Black Friday.

Thanksgiving is getting **squashed.**

I think we need to keep a spirit of Thanksgiving and gratitude all year long.

More thankfulness and less "gimme this!"

We need to count our blessings instead of dwelling on our woes.
Giving thanks is good for our souls.

Let's keep Thanksgiving alive.
I do not want to celebrate **Squashedgiving!**

I love Christmas Eve!

The work is done,
gifts are wrapped and tagged,
baking has left wonderful aromas
wafting through the house...

In the background,
Christmas carols play joyfully.

Christmas cards have been mailed,
the house has been decorated with care.

Now it is truly Christmas Eve!

We go to the special service at church.
where my son plays his violin.

Then, we come home and relax,
enjoying family time together with
three people and two cats.

Relax! Enjoy! Be together!

We each open **one** gift.

We drink the traditional Crockpot Hot Cocoa
that I make every year.

We munch on Christmas cookies.

We stay up late watching classic Christmas movies.

Oh yes, I love Christmas Eve!

CHRISTMAS EVE

SHE VERSUS HE

It seemed so very small,
to bring a sudden squall;
who knew at the start of the day,
that things would turn out that way?

She had been feeling blue,
wanting to change her point of view.
An idea formed as she thought,
her attention and energy were caught.

He had been working hard,
in the garage and the yard.
He came inside to rest,
thinking a nap would be best.

She came with a twinkle in her eyes.
"Guess what? I have a surprise!
For the neighborhood Christmas contest,
our house will be looking its best!"

He jumped up and yelled, *"Are you quite mad?*
I think that idea is very bad."
"But I've already ordered the stuff!
It should be more than enough."

"You wasted money on frippery,
without even thinking of me!
You should have talked to me, don't you see?
For the decorations will not be hung by me!"

"I needed something with cheer.
I did not think you would jeer.
I just wanted something bright
and cheerful looking at night."

WINTER

Stunned, she stalked away.
She wouldn't be treated that way.
Miffed, he left the room,
slamming the door with a boom.

Oh, such a little thing
can so much sorrow bring.
Both were in their own spaces,
troubled and careworn were their faces.

He thought that she was overwrought.
She thought he was tense and taut.
Eventually, they both calmed down,
and could think of the other without a frown.

From their different spots, they met in the hall
and decided to put an end to their squall;
"I'm really sorry," said she.
"As am I," replied he.

Then they shared a passionate hug
bringing them out of the hole they dug.
Together, they talked it out
and no longer, did they shout.

KAREN SLAUGHTER STEINER

SEASONS OF SNOW

When I was a child,
I loved to play in the snow
staying home from school.

Building huge snowmen.
Having snowball fights with friends;
being pulled on sled.

When I was a teen
I was at Winter Retreat.
The lake was frozen.

Snowball fights on ice
are not a good idea.
I was hit and fell.

I was mortified!
I had a crush on thrower.
He came right over.

He helped me get up.
Wanted to take me inside;
I claimed I was fine.

Then blood and pain came.
Hospital trip for me. Ow!
Still so embarrassed.

Concussion, stitches,
plus, my glasses were broken.
So much for retreat!

During college years
'twas Nineteen Seventy-Eight;
The Great Blizzard year.

Everything was closed.
Snowdrifts higher than my head!
Great fun together.

WINTER

Mom panicked; called me.
Did I have cans of tuna?
Was I safe at school?

They brought meals to dorms
which came via big snow plows.
I laughed. "Mom, I'm fine."

When my child was small,
he built snow forts with his dad.
Great fun together.

I made snow ice cream.
We pulled him on my old sled.
Made snow angels, too.

Later on, things changed,
I no longer liked the snow.
No snow please. No ice!

Two things changed my mind:
First, some close calls while driving
made me loathe the snow.

Plus, I worked at school.
Snowy recess times not good;
not fun anymore.

Now that I'm retired,
my feelings have changed again.
I've come full circle.

Watching the snowfall
with a cat on my lap and
drinking hot cocoa!

Beautiful outside;
evergreens with flocked snow and
trees sparkling brightly.

Concentrating on
snow's beauty and staying home,
I love snow again.

KAREN SLAUGHTER STEINER

THE NATIVITY

Alone, young, engaged.
An angel comes to Mary.
She is startled, scared.

God favors Mary,
"You will give birth to God's Son,
do not be afraid."

"How? I'm a virgin."
Mary cries out with surprise.
The angel explains.

She visits cousin.
Elizabeth welcomes her.
"Mary, you are blest!"

Mary sings gladly.
"My soul magnifies the Lord!"
The Magnificat.

Joseph is unsure.
What should he do with Mary?
Put her away? Stay?

Angel comes again.
"Marry her. This is from God.
Name the child, Jesus."

Census is ordered.
Because of Caesar's decree.
Prophecy fulfilled.

Trip to Bethlehem.
Joseph leaves with pregnant wife.
Mary rides donkey.

Uncomfortable!
Hot; long trip only to find
no room in the inn.

In stable or cave,
Mary gives birth to Jesus,
puts him in manger.

Shepherds with their sheep.
Angel appears. Bright light! Fear!
"Fear not. Joyful news!"

Suddenly surprise!
A whole angel choir fills sky.
Praise to God on High!

No hesitation.
Shepherds visit baby boy.
Savior is for all.

Bright star in the East;
Wise Men follow star searching
for the newborn King.

Magi bring gifts of
gold, frankincense, myrrh. Treasures!
Worshiped Jesus; left.

Mary ponders all
that has happened in her heart.
Joseph wonders, too.

What will future bring
for this tiny child, God's Son?
Born to save the world.

KAREN SLAUGHTER STEINER

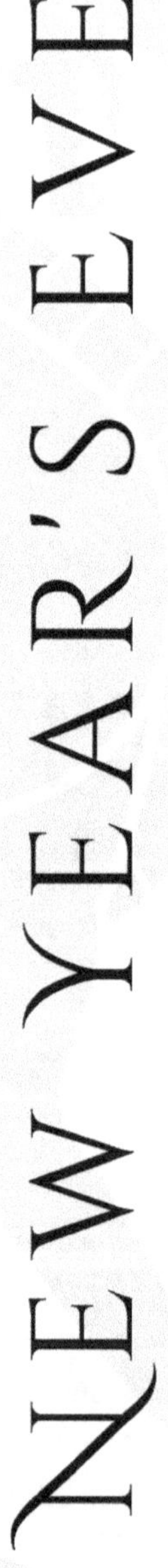

I do not mind being alone **except**
on New Year's Eve.
I cannot abide being by myself
on that special night.
For me, it is worse
than being alone on Valentine's Day.

When I was growing up,
we had family traditions.
We went to the
Watchnight Service at church.
After the service, my family would
put together a jigsaw puzzle.
We stayed up until at least five!
Sometimes, I had a friend stay overnight.

As adults, my husband and I
tend to meet with a group of friends.
We all bring snacks and play games.

I have not heard of
Watchnight Services in years...

Our traditions have changed,
but one thing has not;
I do not want to be alone on New Year's Eve!

Happy New Year

ABOUT THE AUTHOR

MICHAEL SUTTON

Michael Sutton is an American poet/writer, residing in West Monroe, Louisiana. He is a father of three children, all grown, and one granddaughter who is the proverbial apple of his eye. An introverted soul, with a lifelong love of music, literature, and nature, he first began writing poetry in 2015.

He is a befriender of strange cats and inquisitive crows, an amateur diviner of the human spirit and when not punching a clock to make ends meet, he can usually be found with a coffee cup in hand, barefoot in an old pair of jeans and a T-shirt, scowling at errant sunbeams and giving his imagination free rein and seeing where it leads him.

Michael's fledgling chapbook of poetry, To Sleep With Ghosts (an Open Skies Spotlight), was released earlier this year, as well as its follow-up, a collaboration with Australian poet Gen Banks, released in November; both are available on Amazon now. In addition, he has had poems published in various collections, including Open Skies Quarterly, Sweetycat Press, 300 South Media Group, Raven Cage e-zine, and the Dark Poetry Society e-zine. His work can also be found via:

Michael Sutton Prose & Poetry | Facebook

Amazon.com: to sleep with ghosts: an open skies spotlight: 9798415523702: Sutton, Michael: Books

Birds of Paradise: a tale of avian love: Sutton, Michael C, Banks, Gen: 9798361444991: Amazon.com: Books

MICHAEL SUTTON

WINTERED

how calm the day and peaceful, night
when hemmed, is that scurrisome blight
with snow and ice across the scape
that man dare not to show his face

no cars to clog the roads and lanes
no horns to honk their geesed refrain
no lights to pierce and blind the eye
just snow and ice and clouded sky

no voice, no roar from engined beast
no clamouring horde without surcease
for trapped are they by hearth, at home
to chomp the bit with urge to roam

the land, a pristine palest white
which covers thus, unseemly sights
one wayward soul, might venture there
to traipse, at peace, without a care

well-bundled, trundle through the drifts
through piney ways that creak and shift
as nature, wintered, clasps her gift
to marvel at such glory

for halted so, the bustled race
who slave and sew at fevered pace
must now and then, so still the din
when facing frostings, hoary

HER DECEMBER MASQUERADE

such tailored breasts, one must confess

when Winter's seamstress comes to dress

are bountiful indeed to see

whilst laced in frosty filigree

as Mother Earth, her hills and curves

her hips, her dips and swoonsome swerves

are dusted finely and benignly

in snowy petticoated finery

does catch the breath and still the step

when eyes are filled and rapt are kept

by nature's splendour so displayed

in her December masquerade

MICHAEL SUTTON

WINTER WANDERLUST

I found myself taking the old roads
with barely a conscious thought
as if the car knew the ways of days gone by
or had read them in the map of my heart

while many of the landmarks were absent
there were enough left to light the way
and strewn among them
tying them together and leading me onward -
strands of twinkling, gleaming stars
encircling trees and railings and eaves
scenes of reindeer, sleighs and Santas
joyous tidings and decorative wreaths

I discovered a wealth of smiles
that I had not known I possessed
which slipped free along with the memories
of cherished childhood Christmastimes –
like so many bright, shiny bows of happiness
and fanciful wrappings

I was as a child again
sitting cross-legged upon the floor
beneath all those lovely and familiar trees of yore
as I gave myself over to remembrance

delicious warmth and bracing chills
precious faces and scrumptious feasts
longed-for toys and homemade tasty treats
scents of pine and cinnamon and ginger
wood smoke and roasting meats
echoes of songs and laughter long gone
they all rushed back –
to trouble me

they were recollections tinged with sadness
like so much melancholy tinsel
for only in my mind's eye or in keepsake pictures
would I see these sights, these faces again
yet I welcomed them just the same
and perhaps, all the more for that
tears of uncounted joys and sorrows
both flow freely down lingering cheeks after all

I drove onward
warmed by vented waves of heat
and ephemeral embraces

the hours passed and the road stretched along
the radio offered up its Yuletide songs
as here and there I slowed and stopped to see
houses filled all at once
with both strangers and memories

finally, as dusk gave way to night
and the stars above came shining bright
the snow began to softly fall
and I turned once more for home
this wanderlust that had possessed me
slipped away like blankets upon Christmas morning
and I sighed and whispered

"Merry Christmas"

MICHAEL SUTTON

SEASONAL SOLILOQUY

what does one do
when they long for Autumn
and fear the following Winter?

when Summer nears its end
and the knowledge sinks in
that soon comes a season of succor
and on its heels
something other?

how haunted might that man's eyes be?

the snows may be white
and the flakes fall at peace
but the cold that consumes
to make one's breath cease?

when the drifter meets the drift
in its mountainous snowy shift
without shelter from the coming storm?

one supposes the harvest before
need not be bitter
and in its riotous colours
of bright golds and deep reds
might lend some measure of peace
to a forlorn heart and weary head.

are not the smokes
from the fires of Autumn
heady things indeed?

and if he could keep his thoughts from the snows
and ignore the ill wind that blows,
putting far from his mind
the wicked that this way comes?

and the knowledge aforethought
that soon he will come undone?

perhaps he might enjoy
his time in that Autumnal sun.

the fall of a man need not be a harsh thing
and the long, cold, dark night that follows...

perhaps Hamlet was onto something
when he spoke of sleep and dream.

MICHAEL SUTTON

the fey, the fey
came out to play
'neath a full harvest moon

they danced and they sang
they scampered and swang
in ones and threes and twos

the halls had all emptied
the doors all flung open
for King Oberon and Queen Titania had spoken
for the harvest had come and the cycle was done
the great fast now would soon be broken

let revelries and reveries both now commence
with the circle of the wee mushroom fence
for within the ring of faerie to bring
a song and dance of celebration

THE FAIRY DANCE

WINTER

MICHAEL SUTTON

SEPTEMBER AND THE SIEGE THAT WAS BROKEN

I scowl at the Sun
through the window of my shelter
through the window into Her realm
through the windowed pain
of my near indifference

near but not quite
for I have not forgotten
Her regard

as I have not forgotten
the days of my youth
when I ran swift beneath Her
and drew strength from Her sweet kiss

as I have not forgotten
the days of adulthood
when She sought to sap my strength
and Her kiss turned to burning

as I cannot now forget
these grey and elder days
whilst I bide my time impatiently
waiting...

I count the days
as I cleave to the nights
waiting and longing
longing and waiting

soon Her season of Summer
will be done
soon Her powers shall wane
Her reach shall be limited
and Her kiss will lose its sting

soon the clouds shall accumulate
in a spell of overcasting
and the winds will turn
both cool and sweet

and the leaves of the trees
shall become emblazoned instead
in fiery crimsons in burnished oranges
and in mellowed golds

taunting Her
with beauty and passions captured
as they wave their cloaks
of many colours
which mirror Her own

their branches shall rustle and rattle
their leaves shall bristle and take flight to fall
but not before dancing with riotous jubilation
partnered with the very spirits of the air

Her time is done
for a time
and so, too
soon shall theirs be

but the last hurrah and laugh
are theirs
as She hides Her face in shame
and jealousy
behind the kindred clouds

Autumn has come
and Summer is done
and I, for my part
can breathe easy for awhile

About the Author

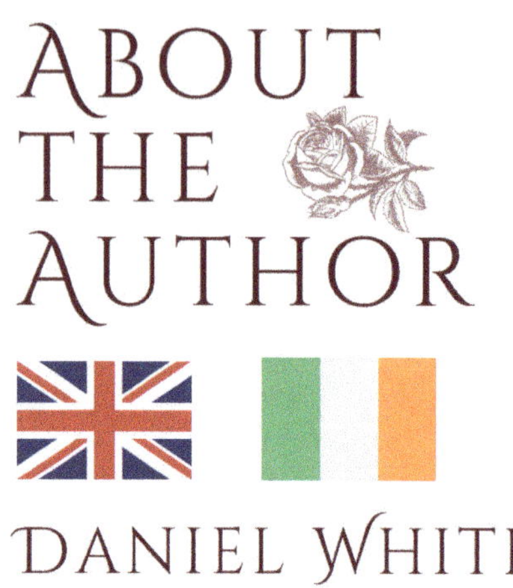

DANIEL WHITE

I'm D.L. White (AKA Danny Boy) an Anglo-Irish poet and author. I currently live in Birmingham, U.K. but my heart belongs to Ireland where I hope to return one day. I am a husband to Lucy and father to Sammy.

My passion for words extends to all forms, styles, and lengths. There is an almost endless list of writers & poets who have inspired me but here are just a few:
Terry Pratchett, Stephen King, Christopher Fowler, Neil Gaiman, Alan Moore, Roald Dahl, JG Ballard, George Orwell, Margret Atwood, Phillip Larkin, WB Yeats, Sylvia Plath, Emily Dickinson, George Mpanga, Kea Tempest, Maya Angelou, Benjamin Zephaniah, Eminem.

Having been obsessed with words and stories my whole life, I started writing during the first covid lockdown. Since then, I have grown a following on Facebook and Instagram, connected with hundreds of other poets, writers and creators, performed on stage and released 4 books. I consider myself an emerging author having published two collections of poetry and prose in 2021, as well as two Novella-length stories.

Outside of writing, I find joy with my family and friends, movies, and thoughts of travel. My career job is in Engineering, which pays the bills that writing can't yet. I dream that one day, writing will pay the bills. I also work voluntarily supporting people suffering from mental health issues, from small guidance through to full interventions. Having faced my fair share of demons, I feel duty-bound to help others with their battles.

DANIEL WHITE 

TREADING WATER

NOT ALL WOUNDS HEAL.

NOT ALL LOADS LIGHTEN.

SOME THINGS WE LEARN TO CARRY.

SOME PAIN WE MUST BEAR.

BURDENED BUT SURVIVED.

FOLDED BUT STILL ALIVE.

THE PASSING OF TIME

IS A TEST OF STRENGTH,

AND SOMETIMES, TREADING WATER

IS THE BEST WE CAN GIVE.

I don't love you,
I live you.
I don't measure you,
I know every inch,
height, width
and breadth of you.

I don't listen to you.
I know the words
before they leave
your precious mouth,
and my reply
sits resting
on my tongue.

I don't need you;
I can quit you
anytime I like.
Just one more
fix, though
for the road.
then I'm gone

LIVE YOU

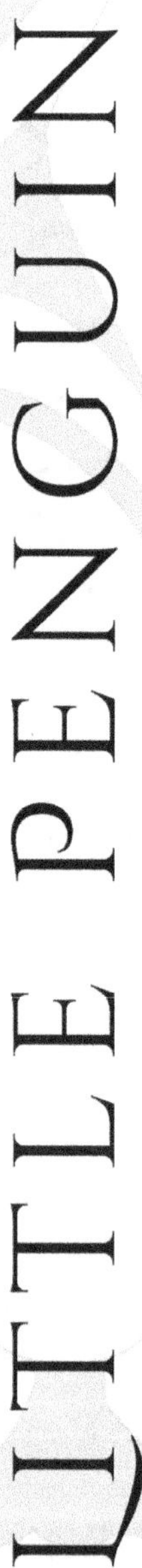

Inhale.
Exhale.
Today, like all the hardest days,
I can't remember how to breathe.
I'm never sure if I've forgotten how—
in deep-rooted, rotting sorrow—
or, if my sub-conscience somehow,
does not want to allow
the simple in-and-out
of chest bellows.

Inhale.
Exhale.
In, feels like swallowing hell.
Out, feels like pleading to heaven.
Each emission, an invocation,
a bitter bilious exorcism
recited from my soul,
interminable notes echoed
from mouth to twitching toes.
The desperate feeling grows
as further inhalations cool my mouth and nose,
torturing my lungs and throat.

Inhale.
Exhale.
Each breath comes as a compromise between
the instinct to survive, and a desire to just... die.
For my soul to rise, softly glide,
through polychromatic rays of light
and gleefully arrive, bright and fine—
to you; again mine.
And my heart;
on these days I wish it would stop beating.
Instead, it flaps loud and deafening; chaotic,
arrhythmic guilt—
pumping blood with discordant lilt.
I want to rip it from the chest hilt,
watch it wither and wilt.

Inhale.
Exhale.

Simple lung expansion and contraction,
that bless my blood but curse my soul.
Time is supposed to heal all wounds,
slowly shine light into darkened rooms,
birth us from the excruciating wombs,
unlock these chains of decaying gloom.

Opposite but symbiotic actions
working only on physical cuts and bruises,
but time being a healer is a total ruse—
failing to fix internal pain and abuses.
It doesn't get better it gets differently worse.
You never fully heal, just get used to the curse.

Inhale.
Exhale.

The moments between in and out
are the most unbearable.
The frozen gap before painful inhalation
turns to exhausted exhalation.
The pause between emptying lungs
and unwanted repletion.
The silence between the ticks of a clock.
Deep chasmic quietness
filled with dread and despair,
where your face flashes my mind's eye,
like a printing press constantly hammering
your visage to my psyche.

You're wearing the outfit bought to match
your sweet nickname.
I was your **polar bear**
and you were my **little penguin**.

You'd flap your tiny arms every time I picked you up.
I was planning to tell you (when you were old enough) that
Polar Bears and Penguins don't come from the same place.
But that was a long way off; you were still so teeny and new.

Inhale.
Exhale.

How many more times should I bother to breathe?

Ten times for each precious toe;
Ten more times - for each delicate finger;
Fifty times for each long eyelash framing Irish blue eyes;
A hundred more - for the fair hairs on the brows;
A thousand times for each hair on your soft head;

Or,
Two times for all the things that came in pairs;
Two ears with luscious little lobes.
Two nostrils with genetic flare.
Two eyes blue like mine.
Two chubby legs, I could just munch.
Two feet with curling toes.
Two little gloves on two little hands.
Two arms always flapping.
Two minutes until the blue lights.
Two hours until the doctors gave up.
Two grannies with broken hearts.
Two grandads waiting in the sky.
And two little dimples
In two little cheeks.

One for each month you were ours.

Inhale.
Exhale.

The idea of creating a new ending,
one in which I cease breathing,
is always appealing—
always calling.
You're always calling,
I'm always falling...

The thought keeps bleating,
and the desire is unrelenting,
to hold you,

'*my little penguin*'.

One more time.

**An angel still has wings
even if they cannot fly.**

WEIGHTLESS

 Today, I assembled household objects which added up to the same mass as you...

...and I held them tightly against my chest...

**...just so I could reminisce
your weight in my arms.**

I had no way to recreate your breaths,
but could still visualize them rising and falling your tiny sternum. I could hear the purring so clearly, and the rasps of your sometimes struggled breathing.

Your little lashes and their unconscious quiver; making me wonder what dreams a teeny thing could be dreaming. I wonder if dreams exist where you are - wherever you are.

Your skin; I swear I felt your skin against my fingertips and forehead, as vivid as the days I actually did.

Your smell hit my nasal cavity just as if you were really there, sweetness intoxicating my soul.

The weight of you was enough to bring it all back.

As I tasted the tears fall into my mouth, it was a smile they met—which made me guilty: smiling doesn't seem the right thing to do, but it is nether-the-less what I did.
I smiled and remembered.

*I wish your weight was with us,
or I could be weightless with you.*

Everything is grey. Not
shades, just... grey.
One aching, soulless void.
Except you; you are in

colour.

Again,
your **stolen wings**
weigh heavy on my mind.

Why should your life have been so brief and flightless,
whilst I throw stone after stone at this endless
swamp of sorrow?

My pithy therapist urges me to find gratitude for the
time we had, which is vacant because it's worse when
I start to feel better.

Happiness,
is the monster under my fragile bed
where guilt lies waiting to strike—
where your disapproving shadow casts subtle
darkness over smiles,
where healing holds hopeless hands for short hours,
letting go in the long dead of night.

Virtue seems sinful;
each kind act tainted by tragedy,
gestures empty and hollow,
conscientious pursuits misplaced against sadness,
all shades of love painted pale by your empty spaces.

*I dare not take flight
when your wings never unfurled.*

*I dare not show hope
when you knew no such thing.*

*I dare not stop mourning
when all I have left is how your absence feels.*

NUMB,
my secret sweet spot;
neither glad of the life before me,
nor sad of the one taken.

Floating with storm clouds,
frightened of their thunder,
resigned to their rain.

Existing,
(in a sense)
between what's lost and what remains—
facing neither with courage,
wanting both to end.

*Deathly grey hues hold safer views
than life's colour.*

NEVER RETURNED

I tried writing about you—
the syllables became my grief;
about how you never flew
but I only spelled out my misery.

I tried bleeding you onto pages;
all that flowed was self-pity.
I tried portraying your precious face;
all I described was agony.

I can't show you to the world
because all they see is melancholy—
I showed someone your photograph,
all they saw was tragedy.

I need to scream;
tell them you are more than my sad story,
worth more than my sorrow—
more than their sympathy.

I want to explain
how you were softer than anything I'd ever known
yet,
your memory is harder than stone—
how you brought me joy in
every short-lived breath
but,
they just said,
"sorry for your loss."

That is how you are defined:
framed by loss,
known by grieving words,
remembered in fallen tears,
seen only as death and mourning.

Not by your own beating heart
which fluttered against mine.

The wakening in your lapis eyes
that pierced me like no others.
Nor by the flapping of your arms
when you first knew me as father
from the others.

I didn't lose you;
you were stolen—
the thief sits on a throne in paradise
excused by original sin.
Or,
perhaps no shepherd oversees
this bleak existence at all.
As insult to injury,
I plough this field of finality,
no harvest of answers
at the end to greet me.
Just this time,
this space,
this life,
to be eked out half-awake,
each second
seemingly stolen from you
never to be returned.
Never to be returned.
Never returned.

DANIEL WHITE

I do not love you
in safe ways,
with clean hands.

I do not love you
in calmness—
seas rolling
freshly spun satin
over trippy toes.

I do not love you
if love is only
photogenic moments—
doubtless, faultless—
not careening down
mountain roads,
wind thrashing faces
frightened, to be alive.

I do not love you
in happy ways;
I love you aching
and mortified—
stripped bare
clueless and scared.
I love you when
love might tear
us apart,
cast our flesh
to hungry gulls.
I love you in the ocean
on its wildest days;
in weather warnings
blizzards, hurricanes.

I do not love you
In warm ways,
kissed by spring.

I do not love you
If love may
not feel frozen;
shatter to pieces
under the weight
of a careless touch—
frigid and afraid,
that it might
melt away
to Summer's heat.

I do not love you In
wedded ways—
in finger rings,
and written vows.

I do not love you
if love is a contract
between promise
and hope.

continued....

I do not love you
in hopeful ways;
no, I love you hopeless, folded
by the world, stretching
yourself thin, between duty
and grace.

I do not love you
in tidy order;
everything placed
as wished by dreams—
I love you drowning
In fear and mess;
I love you lost.

I do not love you
in living ways;
breath blooming
in eager chest.
I love you close to death—
in breathless memorandum,
in wilting weakness.

I do not love you
if love cannot mourn
the ones we lost,
who knew our name
as a single thing;
a single fragile thing.

I do not love you
in loud pressing ways,
howling adulation
as wolves to
the moon;
bleating adoration
in soulless serenades—
I love you out of sight
with quiet mind,
in silent reverence.

I did not love you
at first sight,
I loved you thereafter—
incrementally by day
exponentially by embrace.
I loved you on arrival,
I'll love you as you leave.
whether finding better
rhythm for your heart,
or upon its last beat.

Should you die, before I,
I'll love you in death;
in soil and dust—
your grave, your ghost—
haunt me, I beg you.
I do not love you
in safe ways.

ABOUT THE AUTHOR

ENYI NNABUIHE

Enyi Nnabuihe, an aspiring filmmaker, born in 2002 in Lagos, Nigeria, is a Pharmacy student at the Nnamdi Azikiwe University. He is signed to Whipik Stories as a chat story creative, and alongside pouring his heart into poetry on his Instagram page, @enyinnawrites, he has published multiple stories on the platform. His works have appeared or are forthcoming in The Kalahari Review, Afreada, Paper Crane Literary Journal, The Master's Review and elsewhere.

ENYI NNABUIHE 

A GRIEVOUS EXECRATION

I stand still, watching you traipse the fields
with him; the one you choose.
Your fingers locked in his, your eyes
never leaving him.

You don't notice me behind the
evergreen tree, observing, plotting,
covered in dirt, seething in envy.

You don't hear my feet sinking
into the ground,
trampling the grass, wondering
how you could be bewitched by his
uproarious laughter, as though it were a holy opera.
You laugh at his supposedly suave sentences,
lifting your head to the skies, catching
your breath, your right palm above your billowing
chest. you see me, I know you do, but
you drop your head on his shoulder
and act like the world
is your oyster, because
that's how we make you feel.

That's how you want it to be.

Flip your hair in our faces
and we shed a tear.

Shed a tear and we tear our flesh,
in your conquest of vengeance.

221

This is your one big, mighty rehearsal, and
he's just another pawn.

Until you seal his eyelids like you sealed mine,
so he's lost his sense of direction,
and you latch to his bulging biceps
so he's got no strength to move.

Until you enswathe him in your love,
so it seems there's no universe outside you.

Then you hurl him before a moving train
and watch his essence wither; the one thing
you claimed of him that was pure and true.

So when he's fifty-five and
he's got this other life,
he thinks so hard of you. Of the stars
in your eyes, the cysts in your heart.

**Of how he can't love another
as much as he hates you.**

ENYI NNABUIHE

Never forget the things they put you through;
the beat-downs, the let-downs, the cast-downs,
their venomous persecutions; how
they watched you totter
on the brink of extinction,
how they cackled to the
solfége of your cries, how they
danced maddeningly to the gnashing of your
blood-stained teeth, how they
upturned you from your ankles and
emptied your pockets, how they
held you by your throat and
decocted your last breath. Remember
every second of their carousal, their
chants of revelry issuing into the night.

For you will weep again.
And they will rejoice again.
That is the revolution they relish;
your ousting edifies their souls.

Burn incense to your name.
For you are your own healer,
they don't batter beyond your bones,
they don't scathe past your skin—
their deeds are nothing to the
walls around your heart.

Like dementors, they merely drive you
to the fount of your demise,
they don't make you taste its darkness,
pummel your flesh with their weapons,
engrave the scars in your memory.

For the hour shall come
when the ants become the molehill.
You, in the lustre of your resurgence, and
them shrivelling in your shadow.

LEX TALIONIS

SEWER OF SACRILEGE

Paint me oxblood or scarlet,
for all I am about to do;
brush me down, bundle me up,
for all I am about to confess—
I haven't been the one you tell people I am;
I am unworthy of the attention,
the proclamation, the prayers, the praises.

They burden me.
They bludgeon me.
They are beyond me.
They twirl me like within lies;
a form I'm yet to transfigure into.

They lift me to their heavens like I have
some effulgence in me...
but I have none.

I have nothing worth salvaging.
I am unredeemable.

Thwart me against the wall, instead,
like you do the others who don't need saving;
crack my mind open, till my meat,
plough my insides—
do with me whatever you will.

Cleave my soul, watch me spill;
for I am the sinner that can't stop sinning—
and you're the deliverer that can't deliver
himself.

THE ANTHOLOGY OF PEACE

It will find me one day,
I know.
It will envelop me in its blanket of
fortitude.

It will transport me to the pearly gates
on the wings of angels.
It will sing in my ears as I soar;
heavenly gospel tunes,
uplifting harmonies.

It will be the last thing I feel;
it will drown my maladies and curses,
it will besiege my pain.

It will be everything I've ever desired,
and all I've ever longed for.
It will give me breath.
It will give me hope.
It will tack my lips and stretch them
to my ears.

It will beleaguer me once more,
with the passion of Jesus
& the tenacity of Satan.

Till my quintessence
is quiescent; 'til
it's lighter than a feather
but more bespangled than gold.

Wonder when was the last time you sang?
That last Christmas you screamed
from within yourself
and purged the forlornness that surged you?

Do you remember the wholeness you felt soon after—
the respite that warmed your arteries?

Did you know it'll take you by surprise?
Did you feel it enveloping your despair?
Did it send crisps to your bones?
Did it taste like happy soup?
Did it yodel like impish elves?
Did it caress your hair so clemently?
Did it smother you with miry kisses?
Did it call out your name so openly?
Did it warm your heart with a smile?

You'll find it in the strangest places;
in the phizog of your children,
in the crest of your lover,
in the root of that novel,
in the melodies of that song,
in the smiles of your neighbour,
in the serenity of your sabbatical.

And when you find that momentous thing?
Oh, you won't wonder, you'll know.

The stars will make you drool
as they gleam so bright
as the firmament dissects itself
and swallows you whole.

THE ILLUSION OF JOY

THAT'S AMORÉ

ENYI NNABUIHE

When the moon hits your gaze,
sends you into a lovelorn craze,
that's amoré, you've found your one.

Let him know where it hurts,
where it pricks, where it stings.

Take his palm in yours,
trail his supple fingers, like gelato,
through the sears on your skin—
let your pulse race in harmony with
his, frolicsomely, like a gay tarantella.

That's amoré, you've found your core.

Cleanse her trouble,
purge her strife,
let her know how much she means.

Go tell it on the mountains,
etch it over the hills
fly aloft the oceans—
to the waltz of the flowers.

For in the rays of amoré;
the sun is illumined stone.
In the arms of amoré;
the rainbows are bejewelled clouds.

Scream at the pinnacle of your voice,
"You are my all!"

Where love is adorned with regalia.
Where boy meets girl
in the thrill of tenderness,
the power of passion,
a beauty emboldening
the crux of the beholder.

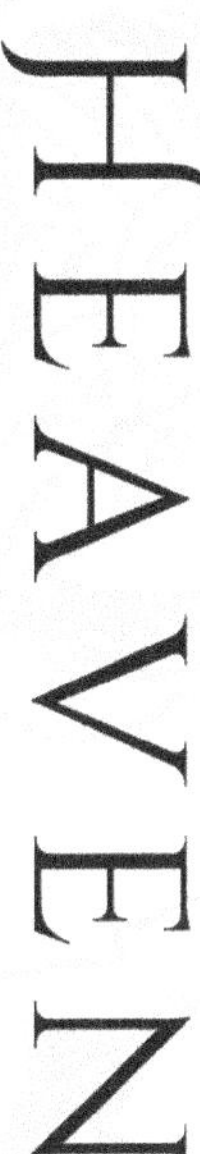

HEAVEN

Ride these roaring waves,
they're the pathway to the paradigm of plenty;
the only paradise you've ever dreamed of,
all you ever wished to escape to.

Where curses fizzle to graces,
where weapons are made of lather,
where memories are premonitions,
and you're the magic in their thrall.

You're almost there—
it's in the stars, light, and air.
It's in the souls of those you loved,
in their rooks, six feet yonder.

It will glimmer when you're near,
when the search is over—
I swear,
it's beyond a hoax of wonder,
the peace you've ever desired.

When all is said and done
you'll be brimmed with faith,
consumed by a sea of felicity
like a prodigal sybarite—
a mannequin bathed in delight,
your reticent self will finally be whole.

THE SORROW WITHIN

I've been running for miles,
been searching my soul,
been harrowing my heart,
been singing for succour.

It's getting harder to speak.
It's getting harder to breathe.
It's getting harder to smile;
to enjoy the little things.

**It's getting harder to persevere in this
sphere I once called home.**

The music is louder,
the people are merrier. But
their debauchery swallows me, and
cages me behind bars of enamel
and sourness.

The sky is higher, the ground is
harder.

When I fall, I don't peel my skin.

With bated breath, I lose myself.

The pool is deeper,
my embodiment is heavier
with a thousand worries—
as anchors fastened to it.

So, *maybe I'm the problem.*

Maybe I'm the evil that needs to unexist.

Maybe I'm the force the
world can't bear to reckon.

Maybe there's a sepulchre
south of here I can dwell in
till the bitterness departs my blood.

Maybe that's my sated fate; for as
you must first empty yourself
to become whole.
You must disappear to live again.

ABOUT THE AUTHOR

LINDA M. CRATE

Linda M. Crate's poetry, short stories, articles, and reviews have been published in a myriad of magazines both online and in print. She has eleven published chapbooks: A Mermaid Crashing Into Dawn (Fowlpox Press - June 2013), Less Than A Man (The Camel Saloon - January 2014), If Tomorrow Never Comes (Scars Publications, August 2016), My Wings Were Made to Fly (Flutter Press, September 2017), splintered with terror (Scars Publications, January 2018), More Than Bone Music (Clare Songbirds Publishing House, March 2019), the samurai (Yellow Arrowing Publishing, October 2020), Follow the Black Raven (Alien Buddha Publishing, July 2021), Unleashing the Archers (Guerilla Genesis Press, August 2021), Hecate's Child (Alien Buddha Publishing, November 2021) and fat & pretty (Dancing Girl Press, June 2022), and three micro-chapbooks Heaven Instead (Origami Poems Project, May 2018), moon mother (Origami Poems Project, March 2020), and & so I believe (Origami Poems Project, April 2021). She is also the author of the novella Mates (Alien Buddha Publishing, March 2022).

LINDA M. CRATE

LINDA M. CRATE

I am no stranger to loss;
my grandfather passed
right after Christmas one year.

There are no more stories,
no more laughs to share, and no
things that can be learned
from his life and his tales;

only memories—

which he didn't have in the end,
as dementia took him from us.

He asked us where the bees went
but none of us could tell him—
we didn't know.

Maybe for Christmas now,
he sits in heaven with those whom he
loved and missed, telling them
stories about us;

as his bees give him

honey for his toast.

ACHIEVING GROWTH

I'm not fond of the cold,
but the snow is beautiful;
yet the bone-chilling and nipping
teeth of a Pennsylvanian winter
are never appealing to me.

I remind myself it is better to be cold
than too warm because I can always
drink some hot chocolate, put on more
clothing, and cuddle beneath blankets;
when in summer one must suffer;
there's only so much one can remove
yet you're still uncomfortable and dripping
with sweat.

They say the water remembers,
and so in every snow kiss and icy whisper,
I am reminded to reflect on memories—
so come spring I can bloom
with the flowers, and achieve growth.

MORE LIKE HER

*W*inter is a season I've always associated with loss, but *if water remembers,* then perhaps, it's helping us to lose the memories that no longer serve us—helping us build immunity against everything we've endured that needs to be washed away so in spring, we can bloom with the flowers.

I won't lie and say that *winter* is easy; sometimes the cold is harsh and dries out the softness of flesh. At times, the gray skies take me to memories and thoughts I don't want to think about, let alone remember.

The *snowflakes* that fall from the sky are like *nature's glitter*... there's something magical about it that touches my heart, making me smile like the little girl I once was— catching snowflakes on my tongue as I spun around without adult responsibilities, worries, or fears;

maybe I need to be more like her.

MAGIC AND MIRACLES

We used to ride down hills
on sleds,
build snow forts,
and have snowball
fights;
we were in such a rush to grow
up.

*I would give everything back
just to experience some of those moments
again—*

to feel a snowflake on my tongue,
and sit beneath a Christmas tree wondering
if Santa would come to visit me;
then, magic and miracles always seemed in abundance.

LINDA M. CRATE

Winter has such
drab, gray
skies—
it is easy to feel sad;
some days I succumb to my
deepest sadnesses, and darkest thoughts.

Fortunately, I have friends and family
to comfort me through the dark—
when it is hard for me to remember my
own light.

They walk with me in the darkness;
and somehow I don't feel so alone
in the agony of my battles—
for I have slain many dragons, but
sometimes...

*even the strongest people
have to know
they matter to someone.*

HOW TERRIBLE

Once a man
laid buried in the snow
near my job,
we didn't find him
until four o'clock;
but he had been there
since the morning—
the EMTs said if we found
him any later than we
did that he would've passed
away.

Makes me sad how many
people may have passed him by
not hearing his hoarse cries
for help;
I thought to myself,
"how terrible to lay buried in the snow
forgotten and unthought of—
how terrible to see people living their lives,
not knowing if you can continue to live yours."

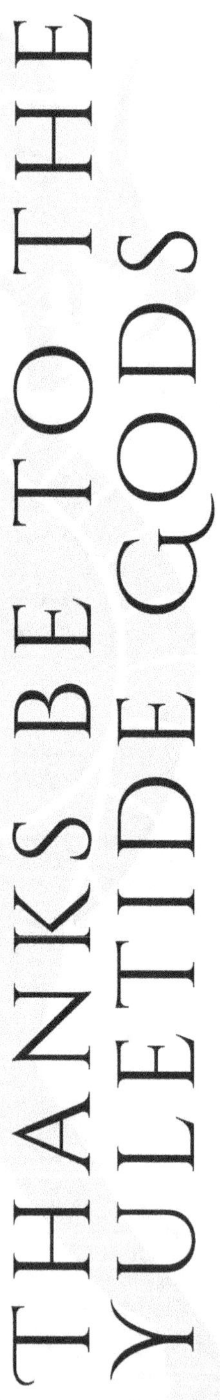

It was a cliché song;
**"All I Want for
Christmas
is You."**

I begged, pleaded, prayed;
**perhaps the yuletide gods
were blessing me when
they ignored my request—**
because in the end
after all your lies, your distance, and
your insincerity I was better off
alone because:

*A queen does not belong
in a union with a fool who
thinks himself a king.*

**You didn't value me, you didn't
respect me, and you didn't know
my worth after all the discounts
I gave you.**

And so,
I no longer wish for you for Christmas,
because people have free will—
and **I only want the people who love,
choose, and value me to be a part of
my inner circle.**

When I was little,
I remember **always**
leaving cookies and milk
out for Santa.

I never really remember
wanting anything in particular
that anyone else would find
special—I just wanted the usual
trinkets and toys—
but every Christmas I was
happy for the things I received
that were actually **"me."**
(Because *sometimes*, people
missed the mark and didn't seem
to understand me, or my style
or my wants).
When I got the book, or outfit,
or toy that I wanted, it always made me
feel happy.

I was and am always happiest when
giving gifts, though,
the joy of others warms me.

THE JOY OF OTHERS

About the Author

SHAWN P. LEHTO

My name is Shawn P Lehto. I was born and raised in Torrance, CA, and currently reside in Harbor City, Ca. As an occupation I am a delivery driver for Stellant Systems, an aerospace company in Torrance, Ca. I write poems/lyrics to ease what's going on in my mind.

My book is titled *Strangers' Voices in my Head*. With the subtitle of A journey through what made me who I am from my mind. As the subtitle suggests, it's a collection of poems written from my 1st one at age 16 titled The Stranger, all the way up until the present. It chronicles my struggles as a teenager, to a young adult, to what I am now. A lot of the poems are on the darker/depressing side, but I have included some lighter ones too. The biggest thing I hope to get out of this is that people will read my words and relate them to themselves for something they've experienced or seen.

I post all my latest poems on Instagram if anyone wants to follow me there @shawnlehto.lonewolfpoetry

My book can be found online wherever you purchase books. Amazon/Barnes and Noble, etc.

SHAWN P. LEHTO

SHAWN P. LEHTO

WINTER'S APPRECIATION

The winds bring the storm clouds into view—
winter's rage shall start anew;
lightning and thunder reverberate in my head;
"the gods must be angry," someone once said.
The fury of the tide as the rain hastily falls;
life as we know it comes slowly to a crawl.

Rapidly we escape to the shelter, alee—
that may be for others, but never for me;
I crave the rage that winter does bring—
to mine own ears, it's like a lonely bell's ring.
A peace comes over my restless soul
within the gloom and darkness, I revoke my control.

Three months of bliss and temperatures chill,
(less of my resolve for the sun to kill).
The other three seasons bring forth my wrath;
the heat and bustle of crowds, cloud my path.
I'm *craving* for the weather to cancel made plans—
for in my seclusion is where I began.

Most find the winter
brings depression to rise.
I find it to be the
season's best prize!

Can't go out too much, it's dangerous to drive,
so alone in my hovel, I silently thrive;
where my thoughts will struggle to survive,
and old memories will stoke the fires, to be alive.

December to February, those three months of the year;
encompassing the darkness that most others fear.
Some will embrace its holiday cheer—
away from that nonsense, I casually steer.

I yearn for the times when the clouds open up,
and drink my whiskey from an old coffee cup;
it keeps me warm as outside temps will drop—
I state aloud, "May this weather never stop!"

Walk among it, the rain, sleet, and snow;
as you're crying softly, no one is to know—
it washes away any trace of your tears,
until it ends, you're in the clear.

Don't be in a rush for winter to end,
appreciate its beauty as you would a friend.
The best thing about it is you can always get warm,
and light a fire inside, to wait out the storm.

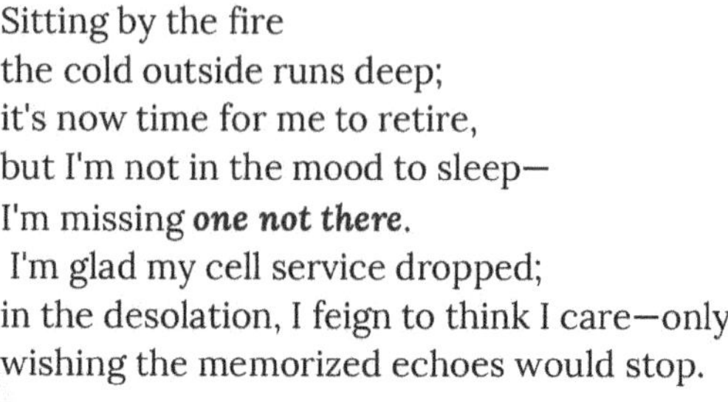

ITEMS FORGOTTEN

Sitting by the fire
the cold outside runs deep;
it's now time for me to retire,
but I'm not in the mood to sleep—
I'm missing **one not there**.
 I'm glad my cell service dropped;
in the desolation, I feign to think I care—only
wishing the memorized echoes would stop.

In the background, I hear my phone ring.
I don't bother answering it at all;
the anxiety that the ringtone brings
makes me more content I missed that call.
It's then I realize, the tone... I didn't recognize
because my phone was in the trash—
it's your phone that I see with my eyes,
I regret the fact that mine, I did smash.

I'm curious about who would call you this late,
but your screen was locked
If only I had your fingerprint on that tape...
the display only shows a number that's blocked.
Doesn't everyone know that you ran away?
And now a text that someone did send...
with a fistful of coin, 'cuz with this call I'll have to pay
from the phone around the bend.

As I'm walking toward the booth
I remember the smile on your face,
but the lies you spoke and *swore* were true
are the reason I'm alone in this space.
The promises you broke when you bailed
I only want to cash in one;
this relationship was doomed to fail,
but I would like my misery to be done.

I turn in back towards our home,
I don't want to make that call...
I know no one would pick up the phone, so I
toss the coins and watch them fall.

WINTER

I know the longer I stay
in this house once built for two—
no children's laughter as they don't play,
I now live fatally, for my time is almost through.
No wonder my texts didn't get a reply!
It's best because of the things I said,
I no longer have to wonder why—but I'd be satisfied
if only they'd been read.

In the distance, I hear screams float in the air,
or is it just the waves that lap against the shore?
I untied my shoes and left them there—my toes
wipe out drawn hearts in the sand, forevermore.

It's finally time to go back in
and get myself to bed,
for tomorrow another day begins, hopefully,
the hangover will stay in the head.
Just to wake up to relive it all again...
why won't the memories just remain dead?

It's been more than a year
since you decided to call it quits.
This moonless night is much too clear,
so on the porch, I silently sit.
Another tumbler of "the good stuff"
before I fall asleep,
and now I know the morning will be rough,
as I realize that I'm a handle bottle deep.

Wherever you have gone to be,
(and tho' you left some things behind),
A day may come and you, I'll see,
but you won't be what's on my mind—for I'll
remember all I've been through,
and finally picked myself up from the ground.
I'll walk right up and look past you
with my head held high and proud.

SHAWN P. LEHTO

STORM CYCLES

Thunderclaps' resounding booms.
Echoing reverberations in the room.
Apocalyptic omens of impending doom.
Raindrops embalm me in my tomb.

Lightning's crackled ear-piercing sounds,
striking gravestones in the ground.
Again, the thunder makes hearts pound.
Only darkness all around.

Storms do batten unwavering shores.
Winds howling through cracks in doors.
Pelting drops of hailstones and more,
coat the pavement and inside floors.

Tying down what can blow away.
Children no longer allowed to play—
locked in the cellar, safely to stay;
silently praying it soon goes away.

Hearing the crash of trees blown down;
branches shatter, children frown.
Rodents unable to hide, soon drown.
Unlike most others, you stayed in town—

braving the warnings about the storm.
Debris does fly, packed in a swarm.
Down in the cellar, safe and warm,
consoling scared children, as this is the norm.

The storm still rages on outside,
all are hoping it will soon subside.
Knowing you are protected inside
while wishing that no one has died.

Suddenly the world is unnaturally still,
but the air still bites with its stinging chill.
Silence eerily lessens your will.
Has mother nature had her fill?

Opening the door, you look to the sky—
gazing around, in the midst of the storm's eye,
chaos ensues as the storm passes by,
knowing mother earth gets another try.

Quickly you turn and secure the latch.
Rain seeps in a hole you have to patch.
You versus the deluge, there is no match,
so you make sure you closed the hatch.

At last, the thunder and howling winds cease,
at once you're sated with the calming peace—
you know the power of the storm decreased,
no longer will your anxiety increase.

You realize now the storm has passed,
you go outside, safe at last;
taking in the carnage the storm amassed—
but the shelter stood up, steadfast.

All that's left is to clean up damage done.
The children run amok, needing their fun.
You feel relief from the shining sun,
knowing you have to prepare for the next one.

ABOUT THE AUTHOR

GRACE WAGNER

Grace Wagner is a queer, nonbinary, neurodivergent writer and artist living with a disability in Denver, Colorado. They were awarded an Academy of American Poets Prize in 2020 for their poem "The Gift Shop at the End of the World." Their work can be found in Salmagundi Magazine, Hayden's Ferry Review, The Offing, Atlanta Review, The Adroit Journal, Crazyhorse, Copper Nickel, and elsewhere.

GRACE WAGNER 

GRACE WAGNER

HALCYON DAYS

Your tongue thrilled me that day,
my cheeks burning
with the words you spoke, your breath
clouding the air; it was kingfisher-clear—
the way the ice coated every surface
like colorless amber preserved
us there, froze your words
in the space between.

A mythbird called Halcyon
bred in winter on a floating nest
and charmed the seas to calmness.

You charmed me, my seas
calmed under the touch
of your gloved hand—I could feel
the warmth of your palm, the heat
of your breath on my cheek.

I can't hear now the exact words you said to me,
but I see them in crystalline mist
between us, fogging the lens
of my glasses. All I hear is laughing
despite the sadness of the past, the ache
of the future. We could not know then
that those were halcyon days
that the storms would come again
and the birds fly away to some distant shore.
But the solstice nears
and I can almost hear you
laughing—

THE HOLLY & THE IVY

Holly and ivy crept 'round my house
before I was full grown, nestling it in a wreath
of green. Of all the trees that are in the wood,
the holly bore my pain, sharp as any thorn. I fell once
into the holly as the sun rose and the deer ran
for cover, leaping over hedge and fence
to some darker place—perhaps beneath the holly
ringed in red, berries bright as blood,
bright as new birth. I stood up, arms streaked
in green and red. The midwinter sun rose
and rose and I swear I could hear singing.
I ran home, deer-swift. I ran home
bearing the crown of berries,
bearing the full-grown sting of youth.
What is growth, but pain?
What is birth, but the sun rising
over a new day, sweet singing in the choir—

HAIBUN STATE OF EMERGENCY: TEXAS

I wake to darkness. Subtropics frozen over. The swamp on which Houston was built sinks no more, if only for a few days. I am one of the lucky ones. Gas stovetop still lights. Toilet flushes with seltzer, the only water left at the store. Outside the world is dusted. Humidity solidifies as fractals on my car. The roads, black-iced, are strange to those this far south. The grid failed predictably. Predictable, at least, for ERCOT who caused it and Abbott who allowed it, if not for the rest of us. They told us "only" one hundred and fifty died, frozen to death or crashed or poisoned or, without electricity, starved of oxygen. As if that wasn't much. The death toll is now over seven hundred. The water, no longer reliable, must be boiled. Now words like overhaul. Now words like climate change. Now words like reform. No apologies made. In Spring, I will discover that the endangered lizards who once inhabited our courtyard are gone.

Tell me, what is left?
Dead palms, brown fronds ornament
desolate beaches.

PROSE

PANTHERA UNCIA

She wanted a pet so she bought one. A snow leopard. But she had a small apartment in a big city so she bought one smaller than a spindle. Smaller than a spoon or a spur or a sprocket. Its coat matched her carpet and she loved its tiny pin-head eyes that shone like a high mountain pond under a buttermilk moon. She couldn't find a cage to fit so she kept it in a mason jar. She couldn't find a cat bed small enough so she gave it three snowy feathers. She tried a thimble for water but it wouldn't balance so she gave it a tear-dropper dripping as steady and slow as snow melt. She liked to hold the little leopard in her hand. She smelled like flesh so it bit her, sinking rosethorn teeth into her palm. Its bite was small so she loved it anyway. One day she forgot to put the lid on the jar and the jar tipped over. She righted the jar and replaced the feathers but she couldn't find the leopard. Its coat matched her carpet so she never found it. She kept her apartment cold like the alpine zone its larger cousins lived in, hoping it was still there, climbing the snow white mountains of the shag.

GRACE WAGNER

NOVEMBER BIRTH

So easily we forget the lost
                    in favor of the living—
November complicates
                    the process, chill wind
against my windbreaker—I am bright
                            as cartoons against the dawn sky,
helping my father, the doctor
                    with our family trade of difficult births,
calving like icebergs
                    breaking away, warm blood
on shoes—he reaches inside the body,
                            cowmother lowing—he reaches in
to his elbow, turns the calf—
                    it is not uncommon to have twins, but this twin
withers inside, shares placental blood
                    with the survivor—now is partly consumed, forced
out, steaming on the ground,
                    a pile of small bones and flesh.

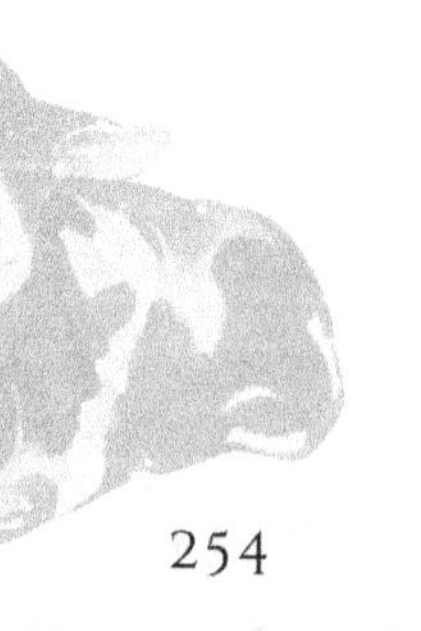

PROSE
CALVING

My hands rest lightly on my swollen belly, and I feel myself breaking. The television cries in the corner, but I already know what it has to say. The ice is melting. The sea is rising. On the screen, a counter ticks up: 218 million tons of ice have melted this year. It is July and our anniversary, but I am alone. The acanthus needs watering and the trash is full. The outline of a foot appears and disappears on my stomach. I wish I could hollow the core of me, draw out a slender cylinder and measure the wet years. I would grab my ice ax and crampons and trek away from the heat of my body, the rotating and writhing inside me. You call to say you're sorry, how horrible that work keeps you away. I say nothing and suddenly you must go. You forget to say I love you. I watch as a section the size of Manhattan breaks off, rolling over itself into the sea. The television explains that this is called "calving," and I am shorn from my mooring. Soon my body will crack, break off, collapse into the sea. Ice like jagged jade rotates and writhes in the white ocean. The foot appears again and I know it is an iceberg, the smallest of signs pricking the surface. I know that the ice is melting. That the seas are rising and will soon submerge me. What can I do to stop this sheering off? I water the plant, take out the trash, turn the television off.

MUSIC ON 16TH STREET

If the violin busker is playing *The Lark
Ascending*, I'll stop for a moment near Writers
Square—If I have a spare
$10 I'll get a crepe sodden with berries
they call "forest fruits," wine-dark globules
enough to send me speeding, wheeling
in fractals fragmented by traffic, towards
sixteenth street—the cinema announces the End-
game and I am reeling towards the skyscraper stitched
by green light, looming over a church built
decades before—I am the broken body
on the monument to Christ's love. Lights flicker
red and blue, screaming down the street
as another person collapses, or perhaps, can't breathe—
under the weight of the blood moon
rising between the corporate obelisks, I realize
this life is hard won and such clarity
feels like a wreck, twisted metal
and steam rising as snow shimmers,
veiling the face of the city—It's May—Mother's Day
and the last snow of the season—reason enough
to tell you to go. Let go of your coat to feel
the cold. Let's go elsewhere. I hear the mountains
feel like home while here the houses
feel like boxes built atop each other, all aching
and none with their windows open.

About the Author

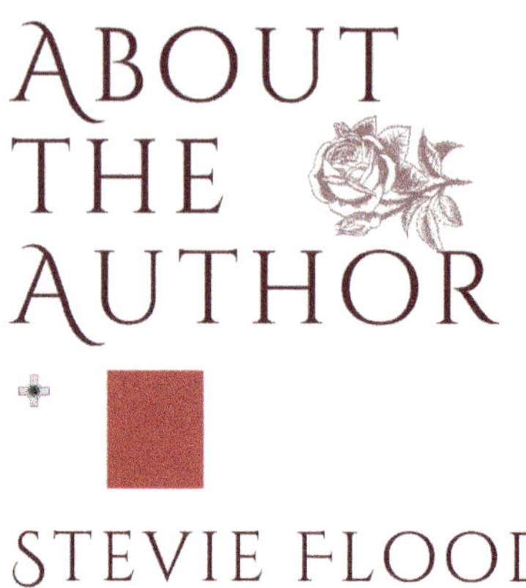

Stevie Flood

Residing on the beautiful Maltese Islands, Stevie Flood has captivated most of her magnificent essence in writing, by the attention of no other than the landscapes alone. Seasonal changes on the island bring out her colourful pieces of ink to light.

At the ripe old age of four, Stevie began her literacy journey. Very special thanks to her father, Peter Flood, who always encouraged her on a whole other level – to be inspired by the outside world around her, and detail it to its very core of how magnificent ink could be, if it is described down to the very last drop of ink, in her mind only then the story will be complete. Making her life as full as can be, these fine pieces of ink were motivated by unfortunate events, and now slowly shimmering memories remain of the man she writes her pieces to. If you would love to find out more and read more of her amazing poetry, just look her up on:

Facebook at: https://www.facebook.com/stevie.floodauthor/
Instagram: https://www.instagram.com/stevie.flood/
TikTok: https://www.tiktok.com/@stevieflood4

- EMPTY VOID
- SOMETIMES
- THE SUN SHALL RISE
- STATIC CASSETTE TAPE
- WINTER'S PRESENCE
- MEMORIES

STEVIE FLOOD 

EMPTY VOID

This empty void screams out into the deafening silence that used to fill this now-vacant home.

The shadows on the wall creep up on me in this distilled space, which are silhouettes coming from the street's passersby. It's late at night and I'm sitting here... just waiting.

The dog is lonely and alone, yet waiting for him to return to me. The thunderstorm crashing down brings me to my wake.

He's gone, he's not coming home to me. I can't sleep on my side of the bed anymore, because I'm constantly wondering if his now ghostly arm will hold me at my waist while I huddle under the sheets where we once lay together. So I take over his side of the bed, knowing that his return is never going to happen.

I stare into infinity constantly wishing it was me instead of him. His clothes in the wardrobe are gone and given to much-deserved charities, yet that ugly shirt he used to wear—remains.

I wrap myself in the fabric to smell his scent one last time.

Creaks and bumps in the house are now frequent. Likely there before, but never paid attention to it. Now I call out his name and still, he's not here.
The air in the room is stifling. And yet so bittersweet, the cool autumn breeze sways in as if it belonged here.

I long to have him near.

Sometimes...

he gets lost inside himself. When the world is too much and his responsibilities too heavy; I lose him to the chaos.

Sometimes...

I barely recognize the man behind his eyes. He fights this war inside of him with walls of silence and gruffly muttered responses—looking through me with distant eyes focused on some hazy corner of his mind—while I sit quietly with my insecurities. And I try my best to love him gently on these days, to find him in his darkness and bring him back to me; but his world is loud, and

Sometimes...

all he can hear is the screaming of his own soul—while his shoulders bear the weight of his burdens. All I can do is give him peace, speak life into him, and give him a soft place to fall—because in all his perfect imperfections, he is enough— and my love reminds him of that...

Sometimes.

THE SUN SHALL RISE

The temperature changed in a split of a second, and at that moment, as the warm breeze crossed my face, I knew that the summer air had heightened to its last. The trees had already started shading to their hazy browns and reds, and I was still waiting for the breeze to change for that one last time.

Skies were gloomy and overhead, the darkest shades of blue. Heavy rainfall was coming, right in my direction. The first heavy drop on my nose washed my tears away, as it gave me a sense of peace. The skies held tightly as if they needed to let out that first heartful cry; bursting from the soul of every other person feeling the void of losing another.

Every sentimental feeling ripped bare inside their gut, lingered up there. Nobody knows it yet, but when that rainfall drops, I'm going to be the one dancing in it. Freeing away every burden I have ever had, and washing clean from all the misery I have been through.

A crash above my head jolts me to attention as the thunderbolt strikes a few miles away. Although people are running around in a chaotic mess, I somehow have found my solace.

I lay there on the curb waiting for the downpour to wash me away. Then, before I know it, I am in my haven. I don't care if the rain sweeps me off—because this is where I'm supposed to be; lying on the leafy avenue, with pure, freshly-earthy scents filling me with the relief that I am reborn.

A gentle hand reaches for me and I don't want to move. The only person in the world that I want right now, no longer exists in this realm—but in my mind, he will forever be alive. He will continue on just as the warmth of the summer air and the blistering cold winters. I am autumn and he is my seasonal solace.

Bless-ed be to the ones we have loved and lost because the sun shall rise again, and so will I.

WINTER'S PRESENCE

I watch strangers walk
through the park just beyond
my window.

Winter whispers its presence
into the air, digs its freezing
fingers into the earth, but still,
people roam the frosted trails.

Lovers, families, friends.

Companionship is a warm
thing.

How lovely it must be to
have someone to not mind the
cold with.

STATIC CASSETTE TAPE

Yes, the nights are long,
and the days are cold,
and the birds do not chirp,
and it feels like living is just rewinding a
static cassette tape.

But sometimes... before it gets dark, the
sky turns orange, and the world glows for
just a minute.

And sometimes... when it gets really cold,
you get to draw shapes in the frost on
your window, and suddenly the glass is
smiling at you.

And sometimes... it is so quiet—in the
morning, you can hear yourself breathe,
and something in you loosens a little, and
you understand the earth is just resting,
and you realize how simple rewinding
that cassette tape is and how much
beauty can be found in a routine.

And if you are lucky, when you exhale the
breath you have been holding in, it will
puff out like fog around your head,
reminding you to keep breathing.

I have no room to

make new memories,

anymore.

I just can't!

I'm not ready to let

go of the old ones

just yet!

ACKNOWLEDGEMENTS

We would like to thank the publishers who have previously printed the following pieces in their Collections, often in earlier versions. We are honored.

WRITTEN BY BRANDY LANE

AUTUMN'S VEIL

*an earlier version was published in Poetica 2
by Clarendon House

ALL AWASH IN CANDLELIGHT

"All Awash in Candlelight" was first published in 'Tis the Seasons: Poems For Your Holiday Spirit. JK Larkin, ed. Red Penguin Books, Bellerose, New York, 2020.*.

CHRISTMAS MEMORIES

"Christmas Memories" was first published in 'Tis the Seasons: Poems For Your Holiday Spirit. JK Larkin, ed. Red Penguin Books, Bellerose, New York, 2020.*.

WRITTEN BY VAUGHN ROSTE

IF MUSIC BE THE FOOD OF LOVE

*as published in Poetica 2 by Clarendon House

THE WORLD IS COLD

*as written with original title, was also set with music by Michael John Trotta under the title Safe Here in your Arms.

LAST SUNDAY

"Last Sunday" was first published in 'Tis the Seasons: Poems For Your Holiday Spirit. JK Larkin, ed. Red Penguin Books, Bellerose, New York, 2020.*.

ACKNOWLEDGEMENTS

We would like to thank the publishers who have previously printed the following pieces in their Collections, often in earlier versions. We are honored.

WRITTEN BY DANIEL WHITE

LIVE YOU
*an earlier version was published in *Works of Friction*

WRITTEN BY GRACE WAGNER

NOVEMBER BIRTH
– first published by *Crazyhorse*, Spring 2022

www.ingramcontent.com/pod-product-compliance
Lightning Source LLC
Chambersburg PA
CBHW072005210726
48294CB00013B/1585